THE TURN OF THE KARMIC WHEEL

Monica M. Brinkman

THE TURN OF THE KARMIC WHEEL

ISBN: 978-0-984-6154-6-9

Library of Congress Control Number: 2010911660

Cover design by: All Things That Matter Press

Cover photo supplied by Monica M. Brinkman

Published in 2010 by All Things That Matter Press

It's difficult to limit Brinkman's writing style to just one genre. Like a well made gumbo, her work isn't limited to one single flavor. The "Turn of the Karmic Wheel" blends the tastes of horror, suspense, mystery, and fantasy in a rue of "you get what you give". Thankfully, we haven't seen the last of Monica Brinkman's Karmic Wheel series. After reading the first book in the series, I want another helping!

Larry Bowen
Owner, The Reader's Corner Bookstore

...I just finished the book! What an uplifting, inspiring book you have written ... I don't know if I have the right words to tell you how much I loved it. I loved your characters, I love that you incorporated E.B. into the story ... raises a lot of awareness to an otherwise unknown malady ... and I love the whole "good versus evil" plot line ... Felt a little bad about some characters' outcome, but so good about others ... I love the poems .. you are very talented.

Connie O., Readers Group

I read **"The Turn of the Karmic Wheel"** with much enjoyment from the opening paragraph on. The characters took on a life of their own for me as each one was introduced with just the right amount of detail so that I knew just what each individual was about and how they related to the other people in the story.

I had my favorites; of course, as everyone does when reading a book...but I can honestly say that each one of them became very dear to me as I continued reading. The story line was intriguing and made me want MORE when it was over. I loved all the interaction between the characters...the plot was well laid out...and the setting made me feel as if it was in my own backyard.

It was a book that I loved from beginning to end and one that I could not wait to get back to after putting it down for more pressing things like work. I look forward to a sequel!

L.C. Danley-PP&B member

This book is dedicated to Kerry Hall who inspired,
encouraged and held my hand through the
months of writing and rewriting.
A published poet herself with
Inside Our Heads,
a wonderful poetry book I
encourage others to purchase,
she possesses a heart of
kindness and a life of giving.
Thank you, Kerry!

PROLOGUE

Few would take notice of the lone figure walking in the early morning light. He looked as average a man as any other, although perhaps a bit bulky in the middle and short in stature. With large, strong hands nestled deep inside his jacket pockets to shelter them from the chill, the solitary figure continued steadfast in his journey.

The sun began to peak through the clouds, casting rays of light upon his form. He took little notice of his surroundings as he proceeded down Pine Street, kicking away the stones and pebbles in his path.

It was spring in the little Midwestern college town of Raleigh, yet it still felt like late winter. The wind was picking up, becoming fierce; a bitter cold that chilled to the bone. Bits of dust and left over pieces of autumn leaves whirled in the air, blowing against his face. He casually brushed the debris away and rubbed his already red and irritated eyes.

Still Euclid Hannigan continued on, pulling the worn, frayed red cap lower on his head; not a great deal of protection from this God-awful weather. His green eyes started to tear and he could feel the moistness running down his chapped, deeply wrinkled face. He trudged on, aware it was another 300 feet or so to his destination.

PART I

A GLANCE INSIDE THE SOUL

Do come close,
Yet not so near
Isn't you, but myself I fear.

Stand back,
Be sure not to annoy,
My outward self, you can enjoy
But not too much,
I allow no touch.

Your world may be built upon joy or hope,
I choose to stay remote,
Away from insecurities,
Outside a wall which blankets me.

-Monica Brinkman, 2009

A HUNTING WE WILL GO

"Get 'em good, get 'em right, get 'em day, or get 'em night," Euclid mumbled, a wide smirk spreading across his fifty-nine-year-old face. No one knew the deep secrets he hid inside his head and he aimed to keep it that way. "Me a friend, me a fool, me is ugly as a ghoul," whispered Euclid, then broke out in a roar of laughter edged with a bit of insanity.

Morning clouds opened, producing fine drops of rain upon the ground. Euclid wiped the drizzle from his face as he entered McFarland's Sporting Goods Store. He removed the cap from his head, revealing tufts of thinning gray-and-brown hair, which he brushed to one side with a sweep of his hand.

Forty-eight-year-old Henry Joseph McFarland stood behind the counter and greeted Euclid with a cheery "Good morning, Brother Euclid. What brings you here on this cold and dreary day?"

Henry was what the women in Raleigh would call 'a catch indeed'. He stood six foot five inches tall, with large hazel eyes and sandy, blonde curly hair he now wore cropped to his head. The weekly gym workouts kept his body firm and well muscled, though vanity was not part of Henry's makeup. At his age, the doc said he required physical activity to keep the 'old ticker' going strong, so he opted for the gym. It worked into his schedule just fine.

"I am lookin' for, er, a hunting rifle," Euclid said as he neared Henry, the smirk still on his face.

"Well, what kind of game you after," Harry inquired. "Turkey? Beaver? Deer? I got the best firearm for them all."

"I can tell you it's big, it's mean, and it gets what it wants."

"Are you seeking dual action for both game and bird?"

After pondering the question a moment, Euclid responded, "If it will do the job, sure."

"Hmm, well, your best bet is a 243 Winchester Super Short Magnum. Not only is it accurate and versatile, it's easy to use and get's the game. I'll grab one out of the back and see if it's to your liking," Harry stated as he walked toward the warehouse door.

A few moments later Harry returned to the counter with rifle in hand."I have a great deal on this Winchester rifle right now. It's going for—"

"I'll take it," Euclid said, as he cut off Harry's offer. Excitedly, he continued, "Wrap it up. Oh, and I got a few extra bucks for ya if you speed up the legal stuff. Can ya do this for me, Harry? I would be much obliged."

Looking directly into Euclid's eager eyes, Harry responded, "Sure, it's a deal!" He never was one to look a gift horse in the mouth, but couldn't bring himself to take advantage of what seemed a very desperate man. Probably needed food on the table as soon as possible. Turkey season would end shortly, but there was still enough time to tag a few of them. No, he couldn't take one more cent than the asking price.

Gesturing by a wave of his left hand to follow him, Harry said, "I'll have none of that, my friend. Come on over to the counter and we'll fill out the documents the state and government require."

"Appreciate your help, Harry, knew I could depend on ya. 'Bout time I fended for myself."

"Not a bad idea," Harry answered. "You'll need a hunting license, and you might think of getting a fishing license soon. As I said, I'm giving you a decent price. And if I can help you with some tips on hunting techniques, you let me know. Those wild turkeys can be tricky to snare."

"Just may take ya up on that offer, Harry. Again, I'm much obliged," Euclid responded.

After completing the mass of paperwork, Euclid extended his arm, gave Harry a strong handshake, nodded his head and stated, "Will be callin' ya soon."

"You'll be able to pick up the rifle tomorrow. Give me a call mid-morning. Should be cleared and ready to go by that time."

Euclid nodded and exited the store.

Harry had owned his shop for many years, seen some come in and go out in a sea of police gunfire, but, hell, he couldn't worry about every customer who purchased a weapon. Fact was, he had given up trying to figure out man's nature years ago. Course, Euclid wasn't one to carry arms of any sort. He didn't remember him ever going hunting or even showing interest in the sport. Perhaps now that he was alone in life, with much time on his hands, he had decided to take it up and save some money by providing his own meat for the table. In any event, Harry knew Euclid to be a solid citizen of Raleigh, a man with a pure heart. Yes, he was a good man and a great friend.

Harry went to the window and watched his friend walk down the street. He wondered if he should be concerned. For some reason, he felt a bit of uneasiness; just couldn't put his finger on the why or wherefore. Aw, hell, he reasoned, it ain't none of my business.

Yet there was something eating at his mind, a voice telling him to go no further with this transaction. It was a gut feeling he couldn't shake, a feeling that his friend and neighbor of over 30 years was not 'quite right'. There was definitely something 'off the scale' about Euclid today.

A vivid image entered his mind. A vision so unfathomable he had to let it go.

Harry shivered as he moved to slowly close the store's door, continuing to watch the retreating figure kicking stones along the road, unable to shake his feelings of dread.

JIMMY AND EUCLID

Jimmy Johansen watched the man perched on the weather beaten wooden bench, hoping he would be agreeable to some company. Jimmy had known Mr. Hannigan ever since he could remember, which wasn't that long, since Jimmy was a mere seven years old.

His family had moved next door to Mr. Hannigan some six and a half years ago when Jimmy was just a baby. Most of the other kids lived in town or in a more residential area. Mr. Hannigan had been the only friend Jimmy had known for quite a while, at least until he entered school last year. Now he had a few friends: Bobby Jones, Edgar Philby, and this one girl named Alicia. She had a twin but he liked Alicia much better.

She was friendlier and liked to play baseball with him. Plus, even though he'd never admit to it, he thought Alicia was so pretty with those brown eyes and blonde hair. She treated him real nice and he could talk to her about anything. Still, he didn't get much of a chance to see his friends unless he walked the ten miles into town or some grownup would give him a ride. Jimmy figured Mr. Hannigan and he would remain friends for life.

He remembered when Mr. Hannigans' wife, Gina, was around. She would bake cookies and cake and make him ice cream sodas way better than you could get at a store. He liked Mrs. Hannigan, but she had been gone about a year now. Pa said it was the cancer that got her, while Ma said it was 'Gods Will'. No matter what it was, his friend Mr. Hannigan hadn't been the same since she died. He tried to hide it, but Jimmy could sense some change in him. It was just a little change, but noticeable even to a young boy. Mr. Hannigan used to let him go to work with him every once in a while and look at the new cars coming off the factory line. Since the time Mr. Hannigan got laid off, he couldn't go back there again. Jimmy knew what layoff meant 'cause his Pa told him. It meant Mr. Hannigan didn't have the job at the auto factory no more.

Jimmy shuffled his feet in the loose dirt and wondered what Mr. Hannigan was up to now. It kind of looked like he was whittling again. I sure hope so, thought Jimmy, 'cause he promised he'd show me how to be the world's best whittler ever.

Euclid Hannigan caught a glimpse of the young man out of the corner of his eye, which sight brought a full smile to his wrinkled face. He turned toward the young boy saying, "Well, howdy, partner."

"Watcha up to this morning?" he asked, as he placed the bit of wood he was working on next to his side on the wooden bench.

"Nuttin' much," answered Jimmy while he walked up the well trodden stairs and sat next to Euclid on the bench. Was hoping today would be the day I was big enough to learn to whittle. Watcha say, Mr. Hannigan? I promise I'll be extra careful and listen to everything you tell me."

Euclid ruffled Jimmy's light brown shaggy hair, leaned close and whispered in his ear "Don't be asking to do something yer not yet ready to take on, my friend. First you have to watch, 'cause whittling takes a steady hand and the love of handling the wood. Ya have to gain a feel for it, ya know. I'll show ya some tricks, but as I've said to ya before, yer Pa needs to be the one who tells me when yer ready to handle the knife. It's sharp as a tack and can cut to the core. Are ya ready for that kind of responsibility Jimmy?

Jimmy nodded his head up and down so Mr. Hannigan would know he felt ready to get on with the whittling.

Euclid laughed, patted Jimmy on the arm and said, "I don't think as yet, my friend. No, best let it be for right now, okay?"

Though a bit disappointed, Jimmy answered "Sure, Mr. Hannigan, but I gotta someday try it or I'll never ever learn it, will I?

"That time will come soon enough, Jimmy, you mark my words" said Euclid as he picked up the wooden piece and chipped off a bit from the corner, before turning back to the boy. "Now, boy, you watch what I am doin' and watch it with a keen eye. Keep these tricks in your young head so's ya are ready when the time comes to handle the knife."

Jimmy nodded, eyes ready to take in all that Mr. Hannigan would show him.

As Euclid whittled away, each clip of the knife hit the exact spot to bring about the desired results. He was lost in the art of the craft, forgetting for a moment the deep despair and anguish losing both his wife and his job had brought him this last year. For a while, life felt good to this kind and loving man, a man whose recent thoughts had been fraught with suicide, hopelessness, and overwhelming pain. These views he kept to himself, along with so much more: ideas that grew in the night, messages he couldn't control or ignore, and deeds he felt compelled to carry out.

At times, Euclid felt himself growing quite mad indeed.

JOSHUA ALLEN

Joshua Allen walked rapidly toward his vehicle, a two-year-old Corvette, on this cold, windy, rainy Missouri day. He tapped the hood of the vehicle in an almost seductive way and reveled in the great job the Mission Auto Paint Shop had done. It looked brand new.

The manager had the nerve to say that red was cliché. And to add to the insult, he informed Joshua that every man over 30 wanted a bright shiny red car. Then he had the gall to ask him to be unique and paint it a classic black pinstripe. Obviously, this jerk had no idea who he was dealing with. If he wanted future business, he'd keep his opinions to himself. No one second-guessed Joshua. If he wanted red, then red it had better be. Had to give the shop credit for the brilliant paint job, though it had cost a pretty penny, not that he had to worry about expense.

As Joshua slid his long lean body into the exquisite black leather drivers' seat, he caught a quick glimpse of himself in the rear view mirror. Not bad, he thought to himself as he carefully placed blue tinted sunglasses on the bridge of his nose, slid them up over his sky-blue eyes, flicked back a stray black hair from his forehead, and settled comfortably into his seat. Starting the engine, he headed home.

What a day it had been! Crazy, exciting, and prosperous, it was the type of day that caused his blood to surge through his body, his heart to pound with exhilaration, and his senses to remain sharp and keen. He'd made a killing in the stock market, something not so easy to do with the economy in such a mess. Most thought him very lucky. He had to laugh at that one. It wasn't luck. Only suckers believed in luck. You had to know what you wanted out of life and go after it no matter what the cost. He was living proof that anyone whose goal was money and wealth could have it.

As he drove, he reflected, not for the first time, that too many people get stuck in doing the right thing only to find themselves full of guilt or remorse over the lousy choices they made. They were all losers with a capital L. Goody-goodies who preached forgiveness, empathy, love and understanding. Just thinking about those pitiful morons brought a sour taste to his mouth. No, emotions such as those were not part of his makeup anymore. He'd learned a long time ago that all it got you was heartache, humiliation, and fear. No one would ever again be able to hurt him, physically or emotionally.

Joshua had seen numerous individuals hold the same type of job he held, yet they could not make a decent living from it. Maybe Financial Advisor in the banking industry was not set up to be the most profitable form of income; still, Joshua took full advantage of every opportunity presented to him.

Raleigh wasn't a particularly affluent town. Most people got by in either the retail or restaurant business, living paycheck to paycheck, eeking by on minimum wage with an occasional ten cent raise every year, if they were lucky. Funny thing was, it only helped his career as people sought him out for financial advisement. Most of them weren't the sharpest knives in the drawer when it came to handling their investments, such as they were, comprised of the little extra money they were able to put aside for that 'rainy day'. Like sheep to the slaughter, they came to him, ready to listen and heed the sorry advice he'd lend them. In the eight years he'd held the job, he'd managed to go from earning a meager $42,000 to over $175,000 annually. To some, he knew, that wouldn't seem much income; however, in rural Missouri, the Ozarks, only physicians and attorneys brought in that much salary. He could live very comfortably, and did, from his two-story stucco home surrounded by twenty acres of fertile soil to the collection of golden jewels he bestowed on himself, not to mention the name brand suits, expensive wine collection, finely manicured hands, and exquisite furnishings and paintings decorating his home. He had no reason to complain, and no reason to feel guilty. It had taken years of hard work, determination, and studying human nature to accomplish his goal of wealth enough to afford the life of luxury.

The ringing of his cell phone interrupted his train of thought. Joshua hit the listen button on his dash, answering with a friendly, upbeat, "Hello, Joshua Allen here."

What occurred next shook Joshua to the bottom of his soul as he heard a non-gender-specific, unrecognizable voice say "You got your money, you got your fame, you got your future of hurt and pain," followed by the most hysterical, crazy, shrill bout of laughter he'd ever heard in his life.

"Who is this? What do you want? Is this Brent? I know it's you. Come on, the joke is over." Joshua spoke confidently. When he heard silence on the other end, his confidence soon turned to apprehension and trepidation. In a trembling voice he inquired, "Who the hell is this? How'd you get my private cell number?" The laughter continued for what Joshua thought was a full three minutes, though, in fact, it was merely a matter of seconds. Then click, and the line was dead.

Steady, Josh, keep your bearings. It's probably some lunatic or a wrong number. No one but his two close trusted friends, Joansie and Brent, had this particular cell number. It had to be a misdial on this nut case's part. He unquestionably was not going to allow the odd call to ruin his plans for the evening, or wreck his weekend. After all, he was not one to make enemies and made it a point to show great concern and care to his clients when the financial advice he gave them went awry.

To be successful and trusted, he knew how to play the investment game, leaving no hint of misconduct on his part. He'd long ago learned that he needed to know which clients were gullible and trusting, to choose his victims carefully, never allowing greed to take over common sense. Unfortunately for the losers in life, those trusting, honest fools, it was their money he finagled. It wasn't wise to mess with the elite of the town, those who could afford high-priced attorneys, or with law enforcement, who could easily set up a long-term investigation of his dealings. He had it down pat. Never obvious or over eager, just a little bit here and a little bit there, so nothing would jump out or be noticeable.

As far as accountability to the clients whose stock or investments plummeted, more often than not an explanation that he had lost a great deal of money along with them when the investment deal turned sour worked like a charm. Little did they know he had invested the money and, when the stock was up, sold his share, letting his clients hang on while their shares of the stock fell to an all time low. So good was he at this game, not one person suspected him of any wrong-doing. To sweeten the pot, he usually sent them a small amount of money, a token to show his sincere dismay over what they were facing.

Instead of retaliating against him or holding him responsible, they felt him to be a good, kind, reliable neighbor and friend who took funds out of his own pocket to assist them, a man they could always turn to in times of desperation. He'd help get them back on their feet again.

What a group of idiots; dangle a carrot in front of their faces and they grasp it without one bit of hesitation. When that carrot rots, they come back for more. This thought brought a smirk to Joshua's face, once again assured he was the controller in the lives of his fellow locals. The Master Maestro, he liked to think of himself. Ah, yes, the one who led the orchestra with such finesse and expertise.

He was almost home, he realized, as he pulled into the long winding driveway. His thoughts turned to relaxing from the stress of the workday; he knew the Jacuzzi's warm subtle waters were awaiting his tired body.

What a fine life, he thought as he drew closer to the red brick residence he called home.

ANGELA FRANK

Angela Frank stared out the large glass window front of her office at the Out Patient Psychiatric Clinic, watching as gusts of wind made it impossible for people to walk down the street without their hats soaring off, skirts being blown above their knees, and paperwork flying in every direction. She found it a bit humorous to watch one young woman play cat and mouse with a piece of paper that continually blew away just when she got near enough to grab. It was rather as if it had a string attached to it, some sophomoric joke, the paper being pulled away as soon as hard-won proximity appears to ensure successful capture.

Yes, this weather was a bit wild even for Missouri, but, as the local saying went: if you don't like the weather, just wait a day or two; it will change. Such a true statement. In fact, it could be forty degrees one day and seventy the next. That was actually one of the reasons she loved this part of the country, the great fortune to be able to experience all types of weather, never really knowing what to expect from one day to the next. And the mountains were breathtaking, snowcapped in the winter months and silhouetted in sun during the remaining seasons. They went on for miles amid the acres of farms, businesses, and residential communities.

There were many places, Raleigh being one of them, where one could actually keep their doors open or the keys in their car without worrying about being robbed. However, with the growing number of meth labs in the area, she feared this luxury would soon be gone. The thought brought her great sadness, yet another sign of man's greed and lust for the Almighty dollar. She'd lost count of how many young people were under her care due to this horrid drug, and they were growing in number each year. *What had this world come to when so many minds and bodies were ruined just for an escape or cheap thrill*? She pondered this thought often. It haunted her.

***

Angela was from the East Coast, where she'd grown up in a little town called Langhorne, a suburb of Philadelphia, Pennsylvania. It was a very small town, but one that had everything she could wish for, in a small town sort of way. Good schools, the local theatre called The Langhorne Players, and fine food from locally owned restaurants and diners. Not like the fast food joints that had taken over the 'ma and pa' shops from her childhood.

Being an only child, she surely received more presents on her birthday and the holidays than most children, but her parents were stricter than strict when it came to responsibility. They made certain that Angela did chores around the house and showed good behavior before any presents would come her way. Not a spoiled child, although perhaps a bit pampered now and then, but, she figured, what child isn't from time to time?

One thing she was glad her parents were strict about was that she excel in her schoolwork. She remembered her mother telling her, "You have the brains to do whatever you desire in your life, so take advantage of it. In my day, women didn't have the opportunities that are given you. No woman needs a man anymore, Angel." Angel was the nickname Mother gave her. "They can choose to be with a man, not out of need, but out of want, love, and care." So Mother and Father would not accept anything less from her than the best. No C or even B average, for that matter, would be tolerated. They knew she had intelligence, and made certain she made good use of this wonderful gift. She was their special angel. If only she had possessed the courage to let them in on her 'little secret', the one she hid from anyone and everyone. She supposed fear kept her from opening up. When she was small, she had tried to explain what was going on in her head.

One vivid memory was of lying in her twin bed, amidst the down comforter and pillows. Suddenly she was transported upward, above the roof of the house, into the night sky, among the stars, and found herself hand in hand with the most beautiful being she had ever seen. Certain it was an angel, she had no fear and willingly flew up into the night, around the town, and into the universe of stars. Such a calm feeling of peace surrounded her; moreover, she felt total bliss and pure love. Eventually, she'd be back in her own bed, fall asleep and have the most pleasant dreams, filled with magical music, magnificent beings and the sensation of pure love. Voices played in her head, sending messages of hope, peace, and universal kindness.

The next morning she awoke, so excited to share this journey with her mother and father, yet when she told them of her adventure she was met with punishment and disbelief from both, along with a sharp slap across the face.

"Angela, you stop saying such ungodly things this very second," scolded her mother. "I'll wash that mouth out with soap. I'll clean those Devil words right out of your mouth. Whatever would possess you, child, to tell such stories and lies? Don't you dare speak of this to anyone, you hear me? Now go up to your room right this minute, and when you are ready to tell us the truth, you may come back down."

"But, Mamma," Angela beseeched, "I'm not lying to you. I am telling you the truth. Mamma, I flew up in the sky with an angel. Oh, she was so pretty, mamma, and we went high up in the clouds and saw the stars and she held my hand all the while." With that, she was again slapped across the face and ordered to her room.

Angela remembered crying until all that was left were hiccoughs as she gasped for air and blew her running nose until it turned red. No matter what her mother said, Angela refused to say she lied, so that evening she remained in her room, not allowed to join the family for dinner. "Why, God," she cried. "Why am I being punished telling the truth? Why won't they believe me?" This she could never understand, but learned fast it was best to keep these things, her experiences, to herself. She knew the truth and that was all that mattered. It would be her secret for life.

From that moment, she never dared let anyone know that she 'saw things' and heard 'messages and voices'. She knew in her heart she was seeing and hearing and living all these moments, but didn't want to be called names, punished, or tagged as crazy. It was just a cross she had to bear. How much she longed for someone to believe her. Mother and Father said everyone would think her crazy for telling such tales, and they knew way more than her about people, so she heeded their words and never shared her experiences with another soul.

***

She had managed to depress the voices, messages, and visions for many years, all through college, marriage, and motherhood. It took patience and practice until, one day, they disappeared and she could live a normal life.

Recently, that had changed; they were coming back much stronger and more intense. So much so she was not able to shake them off easily. It had started out with a dream every couple of weeks, which escalated to a dream every week until she was having them every single day. Along with the dreams, came vivid visions and messages. Words, forming messages, resounded in her mind and—dare she even believe this one—it seemed as if her soul was being beckoned to take some sort of action. Many times, a man and a woman would appear to her in these visions. One she believed was in the medical field, as she wore typical nursing attire, white or blue surgical scrubs, while the other baffled her to some degree, as it was an older man, quite nondescript, with wrinkles and thinning brown and gray hair.

Why would she be seeing these two in her mind so often? And the words she heard were: "Angela, you are strong and good. You will need strength in the time to come. Be conscious of those you meet. Your work is not the work you seek. Be they friend or be they foe, you will get the chance to know."

The words made no sense at all.

Perhaps I am truly crossing over into the crazy zone, thought Angela. So much that I am contemplating telling Monty about all this foolishness going on in my mind.

Instantly, she heard a voice saying, "You are not to confide in anyone at this time, especially Monty. Be not afraid. You will know of what I speak soon. I am by your side. I will comfort you."

The words gave her a sense of calm and peacefulness but also cause for concern. Why not confide in Monty? He was her husband and her best friend. She trusted him completely.

Not able to think about work, Angela reasoned, I'm certainly not getting anything accomplished here, so might as well call it a day, grab a few groceries and get home to the family.

Angela rose from her seat, slid into her light jacket, exited her office and locked the door behind her. The last thing she heard as she walked toward her car was a voice in her head saying, "Good girl. You must be patient; all in time".

MONTY FRANK

Monty Frank resided a mere five miles from Joshua Allen, yet they had never met. Monty was much too intelligent a person to cross paths with Mr. Allen. He knew the fashion in which Joshua lived and, being a successful businessperson himself, knew what it took to earn a decent living in good old Raleigh, Missouri. No, he'd have no reason to befriend or associate with Joshua; they had nothing in common as far as Monty was concerned.

Joshua, at age thirty-five, had never been married, had no children. And, while Joshua stood a good six foot two inches in stature, with dark black hair and piercing blue eyes, Monty had been fighting the battle against fat his entire life. Despite being twenty-nine, Monty looked forty. His short, burly body only added to the problem. No amount of exercise or dieting seemed to take off those extra forty-five pounds around his midsection. Adding to this, the lousy genes he inherited from mom and pop made it impossible to have a full, rich head of hair after the he turned twenty. He seemed to be losing more hair each day. The proof was in his comb. He shuddered every time he saw yet another few strands dangling from its teeth.

Monty considered looks as unimportant in the entire scheme of life. What mattered most was living a grand style of life. This included a fine home, an attractive, appealing wife, and the ability to do what they wanted, when they wanted. The addition of two children, Alexis and Alicia, identical twins, only added to his riches. At six, the girls, who'd inherited their mother's good looks, thank God, were becoming quite a handful. If only he could market their energy and enthusiasm. The girls did get his large oval dark brown eyes, doe eyes, and with long lashes to boot. Their eyes were quite a striking contrast to their golden blonde hair, another gift from their mother.

Monty had met their mom, Angela, when he was only seventeen. She was a bit shy and reserved, but a real looker. She stood five foot four, was small boned, with a mass of gorgeous long blonde hair, and possessed the greenest eyes he had ever had the good fortune to gaze into. A real waif of a young woman, she was. Oh, so dainty and feminine, yet smart as an owl. If she hadn't married Monty some nine years ago, she would definitely have been a professor instead of the clinical psychiatrist she had become. Her choice of profession, he couldn't quite figure out. Why would anyone want to subject themselves to crazy, out of control people every single day? Or, for that matter, deal with so much negativity, gloom, and depression. No amount of arguing or reasoning would change Angela's mind. She thrived on her job and actually seemed to enjoy meeting those wackos. Go figure!

He believed the only reason she accepted his marriage proposal was that usually endearing but sometimes aggravating skill she had of overlooking people's flaws and idiosyncrasies and view their true character. She called it their soul.

Usually a good judge of such character, Angela had absolutely no idea of how flawed Monty's character really was. She thought he helped and aided the unfortunate by offering them a real service of debt elimination. Yeah, he'd end their debt all right, but only after they had to deal with harassing phone calls from creditors, the collapse of their credit rating, and paying him twenty-five percent of their total debt. It was a payment made upfront, as well.

Still, this was a business he was able to perform from home with access to millions of people via the trusty internet and he could be anonymous while making close to 250,000 buckaroos a year. There was no one to dazzle with looks, and no need to seek these desperate people out. With the state of the economy, they hounded him for assistance. He happily obliged, with a signup rate at 96 percent. His theory was: If you don't like what you hear the first time, I'll let you think about it for a few days, then offer a deal you can't refuse. Sign on the dotted line with only two working days to back out of the contract. They seldom knew what they were signing or what they were getting into for the long haul, poor bastards.

It bought the family riches and it brought him confidence, along with cynicism. He reasoned, Hey, they got their own selves into this huge financial mess; don't blame a guy for making a buck, given the opportunity.

Monty checked his watch and saw it was time to contact some prospective clients. He padded over to the expansive wooden executive chair sitting in front of his beloved computer and maneuvered his large buttocks into the cushioned seat. With visions of dollar signs floating in his head, he hit the start button and immersed himself in the world of the less fortunate, knowing it would be a fruitful day. After completing his call back list and signing up several clients, he stretched his short arms to their full capacity and decided to check his e-mail one last time before calling it a day.

The only downfall in working off the internet was the tons of spam he received in his e-mail inbox each day. Don't these scavengers ever give up, Monty wondered to himself while clicking through the 300-plus messages. His eye caught one particular e-mail whose subject line read 'Give them up, rich ye be.' "Why not click on what this moron has to say?" Monty muttered as he brought up the entire message. For one split second, he thought he wasn't reading the message correctly. For just one instant, before his face turned ghostly white and the blood rushed to his now rapidly beating heart, he thought it a joke. This soon passed as he re-read the contents out loud: "Give them up, rich ye be. Got you one great family. They're so fine; they'll soon be mine."

"What the hell is going on?" Monty inquired, searching for any clue who the spammer could be. No signature. *Wait a minute, Monty, check the e-mail address. Surely it will locate who this sick individual is and where he can be found.* Monty clicked on the message, hit reply and then send. *Okay, I'll wait a few seconds and this mystery will be solved.* Suddenly a new e-mail notification showed itself on the computer screen. "Ah-hah, here is the answer," he said with certainty. His face showed the ultimate stunned disbelief as he read: Unable to deliver; no such account.

Surely, this had to be some prankster's idea of a morbid joke. He shook his head, wondering what action to take next. *Okay, I'll send this message to the police; they'll find out what the hell is going on. Think you're so clever, buddo, don't you?* Monty clicked once again on his spam folder, searching for that specific subject line to appear.

"Where the shit is it? Come on, e-mail messages don't just disappear; this is impossible," he stated aloud in a confused tone of voice. Search as much as he would, Monty found no evidence of the e-mail in spam, inbox, or the sent message box. He poured himself a strong Jack Daniels and headed toward the bed to reflect on what had just transpired. Soon, he'd be lost in peace and tranquility, as the alcohol took over his body and mind.

***

As Monty slept, memories from long past crept into his dreams. He saw himself, a small six-year-old boy, playing with the trains kept on a large wooden platform in the basement. They were his grandfather's trains, sturdy and durable, made from steel and not that cheap plastic of the 21st century. He had it all: the stores, landscaped grass, trees, bushes, train stations, and even a caboose car. What a thrill he felt as the switch was flipped on and the black steel train began its journey, tugging seven freight cars along with the caboose, up and down and over the hills of his imaginary town of Steelville. "Choo-choo Charlie was an engineer," young Monty would sing as the train gained momentum and sped swiftly along the tracks. He was the leader, the best engineer of them all, and could make his trains do whatever he wished. In this world he'd made for himself, all the children in the town loved him. They couldn't wait to join in on the train playing. He was their envy, their joy, and their hero.

"Monty, lunch is ready, sweetie," called his mother from the top of the basement stairs. "I've made your favorites, chili-cheese fries, a Casino hotdog, and apple pie."

His mouth salivated at the thought of how wonderful the food would taste. For now, the trains could wait. He had better things to attend to: eating. Food had become the most pleasurable part of his life. So much so, he built his day around breakfast, snack, lunch, snack, dinner, and snack. In between, he'd play with his imaginary friends in his imaginary world. The real world brought him nothing but pain and torment. He'd learned his lesson early when they first moved into Raleigh. Then, he'd been an average weight child with all the hopes of making friends and enjoying his new town.

Unfortunately, they had moved next door to Butch O'Reilly. Butch was the town bully, but nothing was ever done about his actions. That was most likely due to his father being the police chief. Oh, some folks had tried to reason with Chief O'Reilly, only to find their lives turned to hell on earth, parking tickets, noise pollution tickets, and loitering tickets issued at every given opportunity. It was easier to tolerate the mean, destructive child than to dole out money to the city over frivolous infractions. So, Butch O'Reilly ruled the four-to-nine-year-olds with an iron fist. Whatever he said, went. And when he decided that Monty Frank was a freak and a momma's boy, so did the rest of the children in the neighborhood. If they dared be caught playing or walking with him, they'd be outcasts also and face the same ridicule bestowed upon Monty. No one was brave enough to stand up to Butchie, so they joined him in the humiliation and physical abuse of Monty Frank, day in and day out. Monty found it easier—and safer—to avoid the neighborhood children and keep to himself. With that came a home-bound, solitary existence. He'd attempted to venture out into his front yard a few times, but was met with Butchie and his gang's vengeance. They approached him, friendly enough at first, asking him what he was doing. When he'd answered "Playing Star Trek," they mocked him, calling him "Outer Space Freak, Doctor Spock Ears" and, worse, "Big Fat Momma's Boy Frank." Tears formed in his eyes as their words cut deep into his fragile soul. Then the real torture began. They chanted "Cry, Baby, cry. Stuck your finger in your eye. Cry, baby, cry."

The first punch to his stomach came as quite a shock and he instinctively defended himself by pushing their arms away from his exposed body. Soon he found himself held to the ground, arms flung out to his sides held down by four boys putting their body weight upon them. Pain seared through his face as one, then another punch hit his jaw. Two more blows to his eyes and one to the nose, blood flowing freely into his mouth and onto his collar. Paralyzed with fear, unable to move, all he could do was endure the beating. It went on and on until he heard his mother's voice calling out, "Stop it, you're going to kill him. Get off my boy right now, you hooligans." He felt the spray of water drench his clothes and body but also the release of force to his body. Free to move, he just lay there, unaware his mother had sprayed the bullies full force with the hose and they had left, running in different directions to safety.

With his mother at his side, hugging him, getting him to his feet and into the house, the music in his soul changed. Once, it had been beautiful, love-filled, and joyful. Now, he heard the darkness of sound, full of offbeat rhythms, baritone laughter, mocking harsh melodies. It encased his heart, protected him from emotion, and took over any remnants of love, care, or kindness he had possessed. It seemed to say, *Close your heart. Build a wall around all feeling.*

And the young boy listened to the dark music and let it inside his soul where it remained until the day he met Angela. Only then did he release part of it and allow space for love of this woman to take over a bit of his soul. And as their love grew, he hid this shady side of himself, showing only the true love and passion he had finally found with her.

Now, today, as he slept his fitful slumber, the chiding, haunts, and pain of his childhood surrounded him with nightmares of days gone by, stings from the past. The dark music continued its unrelenting symphony.

"Cindy, get that doctor here STAT! This woman is convulsing," shouted Karman to the young nurses' aide.

"Yes, ma'am, I'm right on it." In two long steps, Cindy was out the door.

"Steady Bessie, we're getting help. Hang in there."

She crossed her patient's arms over her chest and then slid her fingers into the woman's mouth, making certain her airway was unobstructed and completely open.

Within minutes, Doctor Striver, an older, grey haired man, slight of build, wearing silver wire-framed bifocals, entered the room and saw Karman attending to the patient.

"Have you checked to see the airway is open?"

"Yes, Doctor, it checked out fire."

Dr. Striver pulled the patient's medical chart from the pocket at the foot of the bed while asking, "When did she have her last meds?"

"At nine this morning. As you can see by the chart, they are scheduled every four hours."

He observed his patient was now coming out of the episode, her body starting to relax. He went back to the chart. After careful examination, he wrote on it and stated, "I'm upping the medication to every three hours. Seems the epileptic seizures have increased in frequency. Now, let's check those vitals."

"Blood pressure and heart rate are up a bit," he commented. "Nurse, prepare her for the medication injection."

Karman placed the tourniquet on Bessie's right arm, securing it with tape while the doctor readied the needle for injection. He tapped his patient's forearm until he located a proper vein, then injected the medication and placed a gauze swab over the area until Karman handed him a Band-Aid.

As the medication took effect, Dr. Shriver slid a chair next to the left side of the bed, sat down, took his patients' left hand in his and asked, "Can you hear me, Bessie?"

The woman let out a soft moan, opened her eyes, and spoke faintly,

"Yes, I can hear you. Did it happen again? Did I have another seizure?"

Doctor Shriver nodded his head and replied, "You certainly did, Bess, and it was a whopper."

"Was it really that bad this time, doc?" Bess asked.

Well, you had us going there for a moment."

He looked into Bessie's fearful eyes and in a low, calm voice inquired, "Is there something bothering you? Are you upset about anything specific?"

Bessie lowered her head in shame.

"You know, Ms. Hawkins, it takes quite a bit of stress to cause your body to react in this manner. If you want me to help you, I have to know what is going on in that mind of yours."

Bessie turned her head away from the doctor and stared at Karman, a pleading look in her eyes. Karman stared back, nodded encouragingly, and said, "Bessie, sweetie, the doctor is right. If you ever want to stop having these episodes, you must be completely honest with him." Seeing the frightened look which flooded Bessie's face, Karman added, "Bess, I've known Doctor Shriver for over five years. There is no need to be fearful of saying anything to him. He understands and wants to help you get better. Isn't that what you want also? Besides, he won't bite. At least, not too hard," Karman added with a small chuckle. "You can feel safe telling him anything, trust me."

Bessie Hawkins turned to face Dr. Shriver and then looked back at Karman. She let out a long exhale, adjusted her body by scooting up in the bed, and turned again toward the doctor.

"Well, I trust Karman, Doc, and if she believes in you, guess I'll have to take her word.

You have to promise me you won't tell a soul what I'm about to confide in you".

"That goes without saying, Bessie," replied Dr. Shriver. He scooted even closer to the bed, looked deep into her anxious eyes and added, "You must trust me. I cannot express how important it is that you open up to me. As I said before, if you ever want to get well and live a normal life, I must know what is causing such an amount of stress that it results in these epileptic seizures. We won't be able to address them and get your mind and body healed unless you're forthright with me".

Bessie saw the concern in his eyes and sensed the care in his voice.

"Okay, here goes," she said, again letting out a long breath. "Dr. Shriver, I try so hard not to get upset, but it's the voices I hear. They frighten me. Now I've said it. Bet you think I'm some kind of crazy loony tune."

"Bessie, tell me, what do the voices say to you," Dr. Shriver asked.

"They tell me that the government is watching me. They say my phone, TV, and computer are tapped, and the FBI and CIA are after me." She leaned in closer to Dr. Shriver and whispered, "They're watching all of us right now and taking notes to use against us in the future. Bet you didn't know that, Doctor, did you? "

"No, Bessie, I didn't. What else are they telling you?"

"I'm afraid to say more. They'll punish me and take me away and lock me up," Bessie responded in a fear filled voice.

Dr. Shriver made notes as she spoke, on a pad he had taken from the front pocket of his long white coat.

"Mrs. Hawkins, you have taken the first step in overcoming your fears, and I thank you for being brave enough to share this information with me."

"Me brave, Doc? I'm not brave at all. They told me not to tell anyone about what they're doing. You'll protect me, won't you, Doctor?" Bessie clutched the front of his coat, hands trembling as she spoke, desperation in her voice.

The doctor rose, took both of his patient's hands in his own and said, "Yes, Bessie, we are all here to help you and you are safe from these voices. They cannot hurt you. Now, I want you to promise me that if they come back, you will immediately call one of the staff. This is very important, Ms. Hawkins. We must react to them at the moment they appear and confront them. Do you understand?"

"I think so, Dr, Shriver. I'll try my best, but I'm so afraid of what they'll do to me."

"I understand, Bessie. We'll take on that fear together, okay?"

For the first time since her seizure, Bessie smiled, reassured help had come. Drowsy now from the medication, her mouth gaped in a huge yawn. The doctor patted her on the arm and said, "Better let you get some rest. You call Karman if you are afraid or need anything at all, and

I'll be checking in on you later today."

Before leaving, he turned to Karman and instructed, "Stay with her and let me know if her vitals change. We must keep her calm or I'm afraid there will be more instances such as this. Do you understand?"

"Yes, Doctor."

"Good. Call me if there's any change at all."

"Will do, Dr. Shriver."

After he left, Karman bent over the now restful figure and took her hand.

Bessie exhaled, lowered her eyes in shame, and nodded her head side to side. In a sleepy voice, she said, "The voices scare me and I get nervous and start to shake. Like I told the doctor, I just cannot help it no matter how much I try."

"We'll work on that, Bess. You go ahead now and get some rest. That medication is working and soon you'll be fast asleep. Karman will be right here with you, okay?"

"Yeah, you're right." Bessie let out a long yawn, repositioned her body to lie on her side, and snuggled into the pillow. Within three minutes, she was asleep.

Karman's heart went out to this woman who seemed more child than adult. She brushed a tear from her face and wondered whether she'd ever be so hardened by the job that she'd no longer feel the patients' pain.

In the fifteen years Karman had worked at Raleigh Medical Center, eleven were in the Psych Unit, though they liked to refer to it as the Stress Unit. Yeah, stress all right, for the nurses and doctors. Many a time she had considered transferring to a different department but felt compelled to tend to the mentally ill. They shared something in common with her: they were all misfits of society.

Karman knew, at her age, she should be married, have a family, and be looking toward retirement. Guess it just wasn't her destiny. She adored men. The problem was they did not seem to adore her. She had always been what her mother called a handsome woman. A handsome woman, indeed. Just another word for ugly. She realized who she was. So her black hair was short and frizzy curly. She wore thick Coke bottle glasses over her deep brown oval eyes, and her weight exceeded her frame by seventy pounds. Why didn't men see beyond the outside of a woman? She had so much to give. If presented the opportunity, she would be the best wife in the world. Like that was going to happen anytime soon.

Seeing Bessie sleeping peacefully, Karman settled into the chair next to the hospital bed. Truth be told, she preferred staying with the patients in their rooms rather than sitting in the cold hallway watching some computer monitor. This was personal and allowed her to keep an eagle eye on things. Computers had their place, but she had much more faith in her own abilities than some confounded machine's.

For a moment, Karman's mind wandered to last night. It was the strangest thing. She had been in the kitchen feeding Stranger, her golden retriever, when she saw a young woman's silhouette appear. No identifying features, just kind of misty and white, except for the eyes. Those eyes, so green and vivid, stared into her own, almost as though they saw into her very being. It startled her, yet she had no fear. In fact, it brought a calm, warm feeling to her body and mind. The woman didn't speak to her – well not aloud anyway. In her mind, she distinctly heard: *Do not fear me. Our paths shall meet soon. You will know who I am at that time. It is destined to be.*

Karman closed her eyes, shook her head in bewilderment. When she looked again, the silhouette had disappeared.

A moan from Bessie brought Karman back to the present. She rose and stood over Bessie's bed until she was certain her patient was still asleep. Karman, with much tenderness, brushed her fingers across the woman's' forehead. A smile split her face. Compassion filled her heart. She was doing what she did best, caring for those who needed her. Little did the patients realize how much she needed them in return.

ROSIE RICHARDS

Rosie Richards sat behind her newly polished mahogany desk fumbling through the mass of paperwork in front of her. She gestured for the young newlywed couple, Robbie and Christina Grant, to take a seat in one of the matching chairs facing her.

"Fine day to purchase the home of your dreams, isn't it," she questioned. Rosie stared at the young couple through white rimmed rhinestone glasses, her initials, RR, embossed in each corner in gold. She had taken on that matronly look. From the sagging jowls and baggy, puffy eyes, to what she called 'that damn turkey neck', she looked every bit of her sixty years of age. Her glaring orange hair, which she considered her best feature, was upswept in a curly bun accented by a small green bow.

Rosie did her best to be well put together, always wearing nail tips of the French manicure she preferred over what she called plain one-tone nail color. She wouldn't be caught dead without full makeup. She occasionally went a bit overboard in the eyeliner and eye shadow department, thinking – erroneously – it took years off her age. In reality, it made her look sort of like a pre-teenager still learning how to apply makeup correctly. Today she'd chosen light green eye shadow, dark green liner, and black mascara applied over long luscious lashes, one of her God-given attributes.

She set down her paperwork, looked the timid couple squarely in the face and said, "I know you believe you can't afford it, so let me make it easy for you. I'll make sure the paperwork can undergo any amount of scrutiny from the underwriting team. The first five years of the loan gives you a low very affordable monthly payment. By the time you reach the sixth year, you have choices. Number one, sell the place, make a bundle and upgrade. Number two, refinance and get a lower interest rate. Number three, you'll most likely have an increase in wages within five years, so the higher interest and monthly payment should not affect you at all. You can keep the property and the loan will remain as originally contracted. Any way you look at it, you win, plus you are starting your married life off with what most couples can only dream about. You'll have your very own home with room for that family that will come along."

The smiling couple nodded in agreement as Rosie continued her sales pitch, saying, "The area is the best, with the highest rated schools in town. So what do you say, kids, do we sign the papers today? Because a house such as this'll be gone fast like a bunny. Fact is, I have two other interested buyers, but I wanted to give you two youngsters the chance to have first pick. I like you. Old Rosie knows how tough it is out there in the world, and when I can help someone, heck, I do it. How about it? You two can talk it over while I run across the street for five minutes. I'll be back and you let me know what you think."

Before either of the couple had a chance to answer, Rosie was gone.

She left the two young adults to ponder the purchase, but she knew she had them right where she wanted them, salivating over the prospect of owning a home. It was something their friends didn't have; they'd be the envy of their crowd. It always worked. If the figures weren't just right, well, she knew how to juggle them around to fit what the underwriting team needed to get the loan through. After all, she was the best realtor in this town; had been for over thirty years. Sure, the kids might have problems in five years, but today they were going to be real homeowners. This was her main goal, to sell that house; make the paperwork get through the bank loan department, and the rest was easy.

Rosie entered the ladies' room, washed her hands, which were dirty from handling paperwork and filling out forms all day. Noticing a stray lock of hair that had fallen out of place, she secured it tightly using two golden bobbie pins, then walked back into the hall toward her office. She was confident the deal would be sealed, come hell or high water. And right she was. After a bit more idle chitchat with the couple, explaining only what she legally was bound to tell them, the paperwork was signed.

Rosie gave the now deliriously joyful pair their copies, wished them well, and set up a meeting with them for the following Thursday to let them know if the loan was approved and when they should expect escrow to close.

Exhausted, she plopped down into her seat, all two hundred seventy pounds of woman, started to sort through the day's mail when she noticed a manila envelope addressed to her. No return address. With one swift rip, a shiny DVD disc fell on top of her pile of papers. She picked up the disc, ready to toss it into the wastebasket, thinking to herself, *when are these yim yads going to quit sending all this junk mail to me?* At the last second she decided to take a closer look. Couldn't hurt.

"Well, I'll be! Someone put a pretty picture of me right here on the front of this DVD." Her curiosity got the better of her as she walked over to the computer, slid the disc into the compartment and settled down to view the contents. She grinned from ear to ear as the cutest little calico kitten jumped, frolicked, and played with one of those catnip mice found in any pet or food store. She could hear the kitten's meow and small growl as it scurried back and forth with that little mouse in its front paws. The tiny animal waved the toy in the air, let it go, and then pounced on it again. The little thing must have been tired; it left the catnip-scented mouse, circled around a few times, lay down and started purring as it licked its front paw.

Such a content and sweet little purr this kitty has, thought Rosie, and chuckled at the kitten's antics. She relaxed and settled in to see what the small cat would do next. Rosie stared in disbelief, shook her head, her eyes open wide and doubled in size. Soon her chuckling was replaced by gasps of bewilderment as the kitty turned its face toward her and said, "Ye be warned. Ye beware, soon's a time you'll not prosper. Listen to me if ye dare."

The formerly adorable little kitty's mouth was snarling and growling the words which had an echoing effect as they were repeated over and over again. They grew louder and louder, each word and each distinct syllable sending daggers of fear into Rosie's heart.

The kitty turned once more, looked Rosie square in the face, and let out the most ghastly growl and hiss she'd ever heard, a grisly mocking tone that reverberated and echoed through the air, followed by complete silence as the screen turned suddenly black.

After a few seconds, Rosie regained her composure and managed to walk over to the computer, jerk the disc out of the slot and heave it into the trashcan. "What kind of buffoon would play a hoax such as this on me," Rosie asked, vocalizing her reaction to this sick scenario. "I'll surely not allow some nincompoop to ruin my day, and what do they mean, I'll not prosper. Me, not prosper? They sure as hell don't know good ole

Rosie, do they? It'll take more than some little pussy to scare the wits out of me. Probably just some sucker trying to get even with me for the mortgage they are stuck with," she reasoned. "Won't do them any good at all."

Rosie shook herself off, patted her hair in place and waddled out the office door, heading home.

JOSHUA'S TURN

Joshua Allen breathed a sigh of contentment as he lowered his aching body into the tepid water of the Jacuzzi. All the stress of the day dissipated as bubbles rotated around his large frame. Ah, total relaxation. He sipped the lemon flavored iced tea which contained a mere touch of mint, enjoying the soothing liquid's journey down his parched throat. Joansie would be expecting him to pick her up by seven p.m, as they had a standing reservation at Courtney's Place, the local Pub & Grill, every Friday night. Joansie, what a broad. A guy couldn't ask for better. The body of a Miss America, no silicone there, the real deal – and the mindset of a truck driver. No strings attached for this gal. Play and lay was the name of her game, one he was willing to participate in for as long as she wanted him as a partner. Never mistake it, though, she had brains all right. She just thought like a guy when it came to dating. A couple of relationships and one bad marriage in the past had burned her, left her with, she had told him emphatically, no desire to get romantically involved with anyone ever again. To her, sex was just like shaking hands or kissing goodbye: the need for some affection and fulfillment. Joshua looked forward to her company, as well as her luscious body and full lips.

He finished off the last bit of iced tea, climbed out of the warm Jacuzzi water and headed toward the bathroom to prepare for his evening. Thoughts of Joansie quickly vanished as he heard the ring of his private cell phone. His first thought was to let it ring, but his curiosity got the better of him, as it always did, and he walked over, picked it up and pushed the answer button.

"Hello, Joshua Allen at your service."

For a second he heard nothing and then that same non-specific voice came through.

"You've got your money. You've got your fame. You've got your future of hurt and pain," followed by a roar of clearly masculine laughter. Joshua hung up the phone before it subsided. He felt the skin on the back of his neck crawl. It wasn't incorrect dialing.

"Okay, buddy, two can play this game," Joshua sneered and pulled up answered calls.

What the hell? This can't be, crossed his mind as he stared at the screen. No unknown phone numbers existed. For a second he paused then recalled *69 should ring back the bastard's number. Joshua pressed the keys, anticipation growing.

"Got you now, fucker." Confidence was replaced by irritation when a crackling, static sound rang in his ear. "You son of a bitch," he hollered, and slammed the cell onto his night table.

Joshua walked into the bathroom and faced the square mirror above the large white wash basin, a bit alarmed to see the fear in his face. He reached into the cabinet and took out the toothpaste, opened the cap and squeezed the familiar white and red goo onto his toothbrush. The sweet smell of peppermint filled his nostrils as he brushed up and down and inside his mouth.

"Uh! My God, what the hell is this stuff made of?"

Rotting, infected pus-filled substances traveled down his throat, causing Joshua to gag as he made a vain attempt to spit out the horrid stuff. Sweat beads formed on his forehead. He steadied himself by grasping the edge of the sink, gagging involuntarily all the while until he found he could not overcome the waves of nausea. As he lowered his head closer to the sink he watched, petrified, as maggots, spiders, worms, and centipedes fell into the basin, slithering in the stinking liquid and gobs of foul-smelling partially digested chunks.

"Oh, my God," were the last words he uttered before Joshua Allen sunk to his knees, gasping for breath on the cold tiled floor.

***

Joansie waited at the corner table reserved for her and Joshua every Friday night, tapping her fingers nervously on its polished surface. It was so unlike Joshua to be so delayed. One thing about him, he was dependable and one to be on time.

Well, thought Joansie, guess I'll order a gin and tonic on the rocks and start ahead of him. He'll show up, or he would have called. She waved the waitress over, placed her order, and settled back in her seat, oblivious to the stares from the three men seated across from her. They were staring at the fabulous-looking woman. Bright auburn hair, with streaks of blonde and strawberry, combined with dark brown hues; greenish-blue eyes, small but so bright and clear; her full pouty mouth, quite a luscious site in itself.

Joansie wore a pair of dark blue jeans with a row of sequins down one side, and a forest green sweater that fell from one shoulder. Fact was, she thought herself plain and couldn't understand why men were always falling all over her. It made her uncomfortable and embarrassed. She wished they would stop.

The waitress brought two drinks back, stating the gentlemen across the table ordered one for her. Joansie politely refused the drink, sending it back to the buyers.

Okay, enough is enough. It's been twenty minutes since I ordered the drink and still no Joshua, thought Joansie. She pulled out her cell phone and dialed Joshua's private number. She heard the ring, one...two...three...four...five...six, and then into voice-mail.

She left a brief message, ending with asking him to call her so she wouldn't worry he was lying in some ditch.

A DAY IN HER LIFE

The bright, warm morning light streamed through the bedroom window, casting bits of blue, yellow, and white flecks of color upon Karman's face as she lay in bed. She blinked her eyes a few times, let out a huge yawn, sat upright, and stretched her arms toward the ceiling. Stranger whimpered at her bedside, his eyes pleading. His master was late in rising and the need to relieve himself was growing, becoming urgent.

Karman patted her beloved pooch on the top of his head, rose, slid her feet into the blue, fluffy slippers on the floor, and reached for her robe hanging on the bedpost. "I get your message, Stranger. Give mommy a second to go to the bathroom and I'll be right with you."

As if he understood, Stranger settled down next to the bathroom door awaiting Karman's return. Hearing the familiar flush of the toilet, he stood, greeting his master as she exited.

"Come on, buddy, let's go outside," Karman opened the front door. A blur of fur passed her as Stranger headed to his favorite spot underneath the oak tree and did his business. Bladder empty, he headed back to Karman sitting in the white wicker chair on the porch. He jumped up, licking her face as a gesture of thanks.

"Mommy loves you, too. You're a good boy, Stranger," Karman stated as she stroked his long golden-red hair, along with giving him a big hug.

She opened the front door and entered with Stranger at her heels. Time to eat; he kibbles, and she multi-grain cereal with bananas and one percent organic milk. Variety might be the spice of life, but not in her household. It was the same food each morning, except if company came. She'd prepare eggs, toast and pancakes for special occasions, but for everyday life, cereal was easier.

With the radio playing classic rock from the 60s and 70s in the background, Karman went about clearing the table and singing along with the Stones:

Things are different today, I hear every mother say, the pursuit of happiness just seems a chore....

Karman, this is sent out to you.
Soon you'll meet a man, at your facility.
You'll know him not by name but familiarity.
Pay close attention to his words, for he is a friend,
A part of your destiny, known not until the end.
… she goes runnin for the shelter of her mother's little helper….

Karman gasped, mouth open, hand to chest, bewildered and befuddled. Could her imagination be running wild? She clicked off the radio and knew, instinctively, that message was for her ears alone. But why, and from whom? Such a cryptic message, and for what purpose? She knew she should feel fear or apprehension, yet she felt curious and anxious to know more. Of course, it might have been the mention of meeting a man. That was a prospect that pleased her, especially the friend part.

A voice rang in her ear, "Time will answer all you wish to know. For now, Karman, let it go."

As she shook her head in an attempt to comprehend, the thought crossed her mind, Oh, sure, I'm expected to just let all this nonsense go without question.

Karman picked up her cell phone, pulled out the phone book and found the number for the radio station. She pushed the dial pad, hearing the ring in her ear until a male voice answered, "KKID your classic radio station, Artie Ray here, how may I help you today?"

"Artie, did you just play *Mother's Little Helper*?"

"Sure did, why?"

"Well, this may sound a bit strange, but did you add some lyrics to the song as a prank or something?"

"No. We have it pre-recorded and someone would have to interrupt and stop the recording to put in different lyrics. Why do you ask?"

"Oh, it's nothing, Artie. I probably had my radio tuned in to two stations. You know how that goes," Karman joked.

"Could be. Since you're on the line, did you want to give me a request? We're opening up the request line in about five minutes."

"No, thank you, Artie. Don't think I'll be playing the radio any time soon, since it's acting up. Appreciate your assistance and information. "

"Right-o! Anytime," Artie rang out in an over-enthusiastic voice.

"Good bye, miss."

"Bye, and Artie, you have a terrific day"

"Don't I always? Bye."

Karman closed her cell phone, still puzzled over the odd message. She had to remind herself it did happen. She might be old but she had excellent hearing. How baffling it all was.

Her eyes drifted to the oven clock and she realized she had to be at the volunteer table at the Community Center by ten o'clock. It was now nine fifteen. No time to ponder this mystery any longer; those people who needed food and clothing were of the utmost importance. Karman led Stranger to the backyard pen, secured the lock on the gated door and headed toward the bathroom to get ready for the food and clothing drive at the Community Center. She was out the door in thirty-five minutes, driving her gray Ford Escort down Third Street, the bizarre experiences of the morning a distant memory.

Wanda Kirklin, a spidery, sharp-nosed unmarried woman, greeted Karman as she entered the large auditorium, with what Karman swore was a cackle.

"About time you got here; grab some of those boxes of clothes. We need them sorted before noon."

Maybe some people would be offended by Wanda's brisk, sharp tongue, but not Karman. She'd realized long ago the compassion hidden within that big heart of Ms. Wanda Kirklin. Under the veneer was a strong, sincere, giving individual who would stop at nothing to see the poor fed and clothed. It was her entire life and her passion. With a nod of agreement, Karman picked up two sturdy cardboard boxes from the table and carried them to the sorting area. Rhonda Jeves and Kathleen Sullivan were already separating the clothing into piles of shirts, pants, dresses, and skirts. The rest they tossed in another pile to be looked at later.

"Glad to see some more help arrive," Kathleen told Karman as she slid next to her. "We've only a couple hours to get them sorted and tagged."

"Yeah," piped in Rhonda, "I'd say you are a sight for these old sore eyes." The three women shared a round of laughter before silence fell as they worked frantically, piling article upon article.

In the end, the food and clothing drive was a huge success. They had managed to give out enough food and clothing to take care of over twenty-five families. Bread, milk, eggs, cheese, and canned goods now filled the once empty cupboards and refrigerators of these unfortunate neighbors. Many winter coats were donated to the children. It was a good feeling knowing they would be able to endure the cruel Missouri winter.

Karman sat behind the long, steel table, kicked off her shoes and rubbed her aching feet. "Ah, that feels wonderful," she said to whoever was in earshot. "These antique feet of mine weren't made for standing in one spot." Laughter rang out from across the room where Julia Beacon, a young, pony tailed black woman, stood.

"I know exactly what you mean. I may be younger than you but my feet are killing me just the same. I don't know how you manage to come here and help out after working your butt off at that hospital all week. God Bless you, Karman. I truly mean it."

Karman blushed before saying, "Why thank you, Julia, but it isn't anything anyone else wouldn't do. I'm nothing special. Look at you, you're a wife and mother of three children and you took time to be here. No, I think this is the way it's supposed to be. Wouldn't have it any other way, either."

"Guess you're right," Julia responded. "Gotta go. See you at the next meeting.

"See ya." Karman waved goodbye, still smiling from the fantastic warmth engulfing her soul.

The drive home took eight minutes, which Karman spent singing at the top of her lungs. Didn't care who heard today. She was happy and fulfilled and it felt downright good.

The sun streamed through the clouds and cast a glare on the windshield, making visibility impossible. Karman moved her head to the right and, squinting her eyes, found a section of the windshield, sheltered from the afternoon sun. Soon she pulled into the short driveway beside her modest house. The barking of Stranger met her ears. He knew his master was home and was eager to greet her.

"Come on, dog, mama's home. Let's get you fed, and me, I'm ready for a nap. That thing did me in," Karman cooed to her beloved friend, again stroking that luxurious hair. The latch unlocked, in they went, master and dog, friend and companion.

She set the bedroom clock to go off at seven p.m. so she could watch CSI and Survivor. Too exhausted to even change clothes, Karman kicked off her shoes, crawled into bed, pulled the covers up to her neck, turned on her side and nestled deeper into the down bedding. Stranger lay atop the foot of the bed while Karman slept. He knew his job and position in the family. With a snort and one last look at his master, he lay back, satisfied she was safe. He, too, drifted off to sleep, dreaming of chasing cats and running wild and free.

Time to get up, time to rise, get up, get up called the radio.

Karman moaned and groggily reached over to hit the alarm off, if it could accurately be called an alarm. A Christmas gift from her sister, it was able to be set straight alarm but she rather liked the cheery voice reminding her it was time to arise. Besides, anyone could have an alarm; she had a pleasant voice speak to her.

As she sat up in bed, the recollection of a dream entered her thoughts. It was one of those dreams where she'd felt it wasn't a dream at all, but something she actually experienced. Music filled the air, playing its melodic tones. A symphony of exquisite harmony she could only describe as pure love. Each note touched her heart's core, enveloping her soul with peace, goodness, and love of humanity. Karman felt as if she was *one with the universe.*

Odd, this dream was about a man she'd never met. He looked to be in his late fifties or early sixties, with gray thinning hair, and a wrinkled, rugged face. A little chunky and short in stature with hands that struck her as being quite large for a man his size. His large green eyes twinkled as he approached her, extending his right arm and offering his hand. As she placed hers in his, the handshake that followed was firm yet gentle. It was as if they had known each other their entire lives and he was welcoming her, an old friend reunited.

His voice, a bit gruff, stated, "We're soon to meet, you and me. Can't change what's meant to be. Together we'll have harmony. Karman, yer my destiny."

His eyes searched her face while he stroked her cheek. She swore she felt the roughness of those large fingers against her soft skin. He gave her a wink of the eye, let out a roar of laughter, smiled, then turned and walked away.

"No, don't go. Don't leave me. Who are you?" she called after him. She watched him retreating without acknowledging her further and just as suddenly as he appeared, he was gone. An ache, a bit sexual in nature, soared through her body. His touch was magnificent, the desire intense and now she once again stood alone.

Karman reflected on her dream. It made her feel warm, cozy, and desirable. She wanted to hold onto those feelings as long as possible. She lay back against the headboard, passion flaring, and allowed her being to revel in the possibility. If only his words were true, if only they were destined to meet, she'd be a very happy woman.

FOR LOVE OF FAMILY

"Daddy, wake up!"

"Come on, Daddy, wake up, we're home!" screeched Alicia as she shook Monty's large shoulders. Alexis then decided the best way to wake Daddy up was to jump on his bulging belly.

Monty opened his eyes, grinned the grin of a proud and ever-loving father, pulled Alexis off his stomach, and rose to a sitting position.

"Okay, girls, I'm awake, I'm awake. Bet we could all use a snack. Let's go see what's in the fridge."

The girls squealed with delight, each taking one of Monty's hands as he stood up. They pulled his arms, and led the way to the kitchen where there were afternoon sweets and refreshments.

"Daddy, I wanna have some cookies and some cold milk," stated Alexis in a matter-of-fact voice. She sounded much older than a girl six years of age. Alicia was silent, preferring instead to walk toward the refrigerator. She knew she would find cut up cantaloupe, watermelon, and honeydew inside the door. Mamma always kept little baggies of fruit for her. She didn't much like cake, candy, and cookies, unlike Alexis who couldn't go one day without some sort of confection or another. They might be twins, but they sure had their own very different ways.

Monty chose to go for the freezer and reached for the chocolate marshmallow ice cream, his favorite. It was difficult to locate this particular type of ice cream in Missouri, but his local grocer made it a point to keep it in stock for Monty's weekly purchase. The girls took care of preparing their food while Monty scooped four large round gobs of ice cream into his bowl. They sat down to enjoy their "afternoon treat" session, now a routine. They'd laugh, joke, and tease each other while catching up on the day's events.

Monty was silent as he took in the bits and pieces of each girl's adventures.

The memory of the odd e-mail kept crossing his mind. He would not be sharing that bit of news with his girls, nor with anyone else. Soon all thoughts of the e-mail were forgotten when he heard a familiar, "Hi, sweeties, I'm home," as Angela walked into the kitchen carrying two bags of groceries.

These things were what made Monty's life worthwhile, why he worked diligently at getting Clients: to give his little family everything their hearts desired. He would do anything to provide for his three girls. He'd die for them if need be. Monty stood up, gave Angela a big bear hug and a kiss on the lips. With absolute certainty, he knew no one would ever harm his family. No one! He'd make sure of it.

"Now off to the family room with the three of you," Angela said as she scooted them in that direction. "Mom's going to unpack the groceries and get dinner started, so shoo!"

Not needing further encouragement, Monty, Alicia, and Alexis rushed into the family room set to enjoy the afternoon Nickelodeon shows while Angela fixed them dinner.

After enjoying a scrumptious meal, Monty excused himself and headed toward his office, his normal routine. This was the best time to find prospective clients seeking his advice. Monty gladly obliged, giving them advice, repeatedly, until they felt confident he would be the only tool to use to get out of their financial mess. Ah, when the economy was in a sad state, his business boomed. From what he knew of economic trends, he would be rolling in the dough for quite a long while. More and more families were reaching out to him every single day. They wanted someone to care. They needed a way out, which he gave them. Only thing was, he didn't tell them they could do the same thing on their own and not have to pay anyone a single penny. Why should he? Life was a bitch, as the saying went, and if someone was going to make a profit off the misery of others, it might as well be him.

He sat down in front of his trusty computer, which he affectionately called Elaine, clicked on his e-mail, then the inbox, knowing he'd find at least ten or twenty people seeking assistance. They were there, all right. He read the subject lines: Please contact me; Need your help; Saw your web site and have questions; Give them up, rich ye be.

What the hell? thought Monty. Okay, let's see what this character has to say to me now.

With that, he clicked on the message. Immediately letters appeared, one by one, eerily jagged letters that grew in size until they took over his entire screen. First a G the size of a peanut, throbbing as if it had a heartbeat of its very own, coming alive, growing larger and larger until it was a zigzagged pulsing black G with bright yellow vibrating rays coming from all around it. Then an I, and so on, until the letters formed a familiar message, which read, Give them up, rich ye be, got you one great family. They're so fine; they'll soon be mine. Monty clutched his hand to his chest as his heart pulsated rapidly. He re-read the message, trying to make sense of it all. Surely someone was attempting – and succeeding – in creating fear and horror to punish him in some way.

But why? And who could it be? He knew he had many enemies. Countless people who thought their debt relief would be non-confrontational and easy to deal with on a daily basis but found, in truth, they were being harassed at home, at work, via snail mail and e-mail by their credit card companies. He would tell them to expect some communication and threats from these companies, except he made it sound as if he would take care of everything. They'd soon realize that threatening phone calls, legal litigation and harassment would be an everyday part of their lives. This was something they felt they had paid him to protect them against. Too late they would find it was up to them to take the calls, deal with the letters from lawyers until it was driving them insane. They'd be left wondering what he did to earn his hefty percentage of their total debt. They would find that he became *unavailable* when they tried to contact him, although he did take an occasional call just to show some concern, and made it a point to ease their minds by telling them it would go away eventually. Which, of course, it would – once their bank account sported a hefty sum of money.

Each month a direct deposit from their personal checking account was made into their *debt relief* account. The first payment from was made directly to him, as were the second, third, fourth, or more, according to how much they owed him. It could take anywhere from six months to a year to pay his portion off. Only then would they start building funds toward paying off their actual credit card debt. It usually took from two to five years to pay their debt in full. All the while they were receiving the calls and letters making demands, threatening their homes, their jobs, and their credit ratings. If they expected a good credit rating, they were plain and simple fools. He'd never, ever promised them that much, but hinted they would be able to re-establish their credit rating again. It took five to ten years to write bad debts off of the credit bureaus, depending on the state the debt was accrued in. Some people heard what they want to hear, not what he actually told them. He wasn't able to change that fact.

Certainly could be any number of people sending this message, and Monty was intent on locating exactly who it was. He quickly hit the reply icon in his e-mail, sending the following message: Exactly what do you want of me? Why are you contacting me? He typed in his name and hit the send button. Confident he had made contact with this person, Monty waited for a response. Perspiration drops formed on his forehead. Taking a tissue, Monty wiped the beads away, then placed the tissue in the wastebasket beneath his feet. He glared at the computers screen, expecting an answer any moment. To his dismay, a message appeared in his inbox, which read when he clicked on it: Unable to verify recipient's address. Reason: unknown e-mail address.

"Not again" Monty whispered as he clicked on his received messages searching for the subject 'Give them up, rich ye be'. To his disbelief, there was nothing. It was as if the message had never existed.

A deep empty sob caught in his throat as he shut down his computer, fearing contact with anyone, and wondering how he would make a living if he could not overcome the alarm he felt. It was as if the computer, once his dear friend, had now turned on him, never to bring pleasure and profit again. Briefly, the thought crossed his mind to report this to the police or to the e-mail provider. Upon further thought, he realized he had no proof. Next time, he would print it out. Then no one could question his sanity. With this plan in mind, Monty wiggled out of his chair and walked to the family room to spend the rest of the evening with his loved ones.

ROSIE IS AS ROSIE DOES

As the sun was just setting in the west, Rosie opened the door of her 2009 yellow Ford Focus. She squeezed her immense body into the tiny seat, buckled the seat belt, started the engine, and pulled out of her private parking space onto Pine Street.

Pine Street consisted of numerous boutiques, bookstores, sporting goods stores, and small restaurants that still believed in serving home-cooked meals. Meals with gobs of down-home specialties such as biscuits and gravy, deep fried country chicken, and barbecued ribs, all made with authentic ingredients like real butter and bacon grease, not that imitation stuff used at the junk food joints in town. Rosie salivated a wee bit just thinking of how tasty the food had been at the restaurants she frequented.

A car horn blasted from behind and Rosie became aware that the light had turned green. In a gravelly voice she said aloud, yet not loud enough for them to hear, "Hold your horses, friend, I'm moving. Take it easy, Christ Almighty!"

A horn blasted a second time, drawing Rosie's' attention to a brown-haired woman frantically waving and hollering out her window, "Yoohoo. Howdy, Rosie girl! "

"That darn fool," Rosie mumbled to herself. Such carrying on, hooting and hollering right here in broad daylight. Scared the bejesus out of me. Rosie held her hand up, waved a brief hello, and continued on her way home.

Houses buzzed past her as she followed Bishop Avenue to the end where it forked and the choice was either turn left and end up at the edge of the Gasconade River or turn right travel down Russellmans Drive. Rosie made the right turn, continued past Ed and Nita's white ranch home, past the Honesetter's blue and brick three-story until she arrived at her residence.

It was a magnificent home, all right. When she purchased the place, it had required a great deal of TLC, being an old farmhouse from the 1920s. What captured her heart more than anything was the way the porch wrapped completely around the old house. She knew with a bit of elbow grease and hard-earned money this house would be her sanctuary, her palace to come home to each day. The garage was detached but could fit two cars inside easily. Plus, it was close enough to the back porch entry that, even at her size, Rosie had no difficulty making the short trek from the garage to the door. Up a couple of concrete steps was all it took. Even had cellar doors, which was a feature hard to come by these days. They were the old kind that opened up, revealing steps going down to the cellar. Seemed to be a bat retreat, though, so Rosie never entered that way; always from the inside of the house. The bats liked the dark corner areas right inside the cellar doors and seemed happy enough to stay there; she never encountered any of them elsewhere in the cellar.

Tulips were the only thing growing this time of year and she was one of the finest gardeners in the town. The flowers graced the area in front of her back porch and all around; all colors: yellow, lavender, pink, purple, red, and even an exotic black variety. They were neatly framed, of course, by a little white picket fence. Maybe some folks thought it a bit corny, but Rosie had dreamed of that white picket fence since she was a little girl and now she had it. Fact was, she had everything her heart desired, except for maybe a good man. That was a difficult item to find. Most of the men she met and went out with would wine and dine her, but she soon discovered they were only after the massive fortune she'd managed to build over the years. *"Just can't trust them,"* she'd thought often.

She carried her hefty body up the back stairs and onto the massive porch, entered her home and headed to the bedroom to, as she always said, get comfy and cozy.

After kicking her shoes off, she pulled off the expensive skirt and blouse, which she folded neatly and placed on her bed. She sat on the bed's edge and took off her pantyhose. Next was the wretched bra that encased her massive breasts. If it was up to her, she'd go braless, which she often did in the privacy of her home. Rosie walked over to the door and slipped into a moo-moo style nightgown that she kept hung on the door's hook and slid her feet into her favorite pair of pink slippers. She entered the adjoining bathroom, reached to her hair and removed the green bow and bobby pins which held the bun in place. Long layers of thick curly hair fell below her shoulders; she swiftly pulled it away from her face using two hair combs.

She twisted the left faucet at full force and the right at medium. Rosie felt the water change from ice cold to lukewarm. While the water ran, she began humming a song, a bit out of tune, but recognizable. *You are my sunshine, my only sunshine.* Silencing herself, she brought out a jar of cream makeup remover and twisted the cap, enjoying the faint aroma of vanilla and almond. Daintily she dipped her right hand into the cream and proceeded to smear it over her entire face and neck. As she rubbed the thick, white creamy lotion deep into her pores, making an oval with her mouth so as to get into every nook and cranny, her eyes nearly bulged out of her face. Puzzled, she hesitated and realized the more she rubbed, the darker in color the white makeup remover became.

"Sweet Jesus, what is in this stuff and where in the world is that disgusting smell coming from?" It couldn't be the remover. Hell, she'd used this same jar for the last three days. Yet the deeper and harder she massaged the cream into her face, the more revolting the stench became and the darker the cream turned; there was now a deep brown colored face looking back at her in the mirror.

"I'm getting this goop off me right this instant," Rosie stated hysterically. She frantically searched for a washcloth and finally located one behind her, hanging from a rail, and began rubbing the brown foul-smelling gunk off her face. With each rub erupted huge red and white boils and welts where the cream had touched her skin.

"Oh, my Lord," Rosie exclaimed, "this can't be real. This just isn't happening. My face...my face!" She screamed in utter terror.

Rosie grasped her face and pressed her palms into them as spiders, beetles, ladybugs, ants, and caterpillars exited each boil and welt, falling onto her breasts. They traveled down the length of the gown and onto her once pink slippers, slippers that were now a murky, muddy brown. Rosie tried her best to swat and wipe them away, yet the more she swatted and wiped, the greater they multiplied, until they covered her entire face, neck, and body. The reek of them made her sick to her stomach. She turned toward the toilet to expel the vomit surging in her throat. Upon heaving and hurling her guts up, she grew exhausted and lapsed into unconsciousness, sliding onto the dense pink rug beneath her feet.

HOME, WHERE
THE HEARTH IS

The twins stood in front of Monty giving him big, puppy-eye looks. It was a look he had grown to know all too well. He stared back at them, awaiting the pleas to stay up and watch TV "just a little bit more."

The twins certainly knew how to get their way. More often than not, they knew exactly what it would take to persuade him to see things from their point of view. Ultimately, he'd give in to their pleas and begging, a tendency which frustrated the crap out of Angela, who stood behind the girls, arms crossed in front of her, a bit of a frown on her face, anticipating what was to follow. She had asked Monty to please be more firm, telling him the girls could twist him around their tiny fingers, then she'd laugh her harmonic laugh, letting him know she understood. Later, he knew they'd have a long chat about raising a child responsibly.

How she could resist their adorable, sweet faces was a mystery to him. He'd been trying to do so for years. Eighty percent of the time, he failed. It was not a very good track record for a responsible father, he supposed. As he'd predicted, Alexis started in with, "Daddy, pleeeze can we watch one more show? We're not tired and we've waited all week to see *Idyllic American Singer*. We looove Mandy. She is so cool!" Of course, she was referring to the Idyllic Singer the girls preferred this season. Immediately Alicia chimed in with, "Pleeeze, Daddy, please? Of course, it worked, just as these golden-haired young girls knew it would.

"Okay," said Monty, "but only this one show and then off to bed with the two of you, is that a deal?

"Oh, thank you, Daddy, we love you, Daddy," sang the girls as they hung onto Monty's legs and gave them a huge hug. Angela shook her head and gave Monty another one of her looks. It was not quite of approval or disapproval, more of *they got to you again. She* walked over to the couch, sat down, squeezing in next to Alexis who had already settled beside her sister and dad to enjoy the show.

This is what I live for, Monty again reflected as he draped his arm against the back of the sofa, savoring the moment of closeness and love in his small family. "I am a very lucky guy," he said aloud, the three females shushing him as Mandy took the stage.

After the show was over, as agreed, the twins followed Angela to their room. She tucked them in, kissing both on the forehead, whispering "Goodnight, Sweetie" into their ears.

Alexis fell instantly to sleep, but not so her twin.

"What's up, Alish? Can't sleep," asked Angela, turning toward the wide awake and alert child.

"Mommy, read me a story. I'm not a bit tired," said Alicia peering at Angela with persuasive eyes as she sat upright beneath the down comforter covering her single bed.

"Honey," answered Angela, "your sister is asleep. We don't want to wake her, now do we?"

"Well, I guess not, Mommy, but will I fall asleep then?" replied Alicia as she slid further under the thick white, covers pulling them up over her small shoulders.

"Tell you what, sweetie. Lie back, cuddle up under the covers, close your eyes and think of something that makes you feel happy"

"Like what, Mommy"?

"Anything you like at all. It could be ice cream cones, a new kitty cat, our dog Gumption, singing your favorite song. It can be anything you love. All you do is close your eyes, picture it in your mind, and think about it. "

"Worth a try, I s'pose," said Alicia as she let out a long yawn, stretched her arms out over the covers and assumed the very comfortable fetal position. "I'm gonna think about you, Mommy. Will that be okay?

"Of course, Alish, I would like that very much," Angela answered as she bent over and placed a kiss on Alisha's forehead.

"Now shush," said Angela bringing her finger to her lips, hushing any further questions or talk Alicia might have.

"Get some sleep. Before you know it, you'll be dreaming wonderful dreams and waking up to a gorgeous new day. Tomorrow is Saturday. How about I make us some blueberry pancakes? Would you like that, Alish?"

"Yes, Mommy, I'd love blueberry pancakes. Maybe I'll think about them instead of you. Would that be okay?"

Laughing at her child's truthfulness and innocence, Angela nodded yes and cooed a "Goodnight, sweetie," as she left her daughters' room, closing the door securely behind her.

As she passed the family room, Angela peeked in, only to view Monty fast asleep and snoring. She tiptoed over to him and placed the couch throw over his large body, tucking it in underneath his legs while pulling it up over his massive chest. He stirred slightly and groaned that sensual male groan most wives find familiar, turned on his side and started in again with the deep snoring. With that, Angela headed up the stairs to get herself ready for bed.

After brushing her teeth, washing her face, and combing her long hair, Angela slipped into her lilac-colored nightgown, the one with tiny pearl and ribbon flowers cascading down the front, pulled back the blue and white checked bedspread, and crawled into bed. While she settled in beneath the covers, a voice whispered into her ear, "Angela, I am here by your side." Angela groaned, partially in acknowledgment, partially in rejection, and wholeheartedly in exasperation, wondering why she had to be different. She wasn't able to tune the voice out recently. No matter what she tried, ignoring it, dismissing it, her tactics failed. In fact, it seemed the more she resisted, the more often the voice would return.

"Who are you? "What do you want of me? Can't you just let me be and leave me alone?"

A soft voice answered, "I am goodness, I am innocence, I am virtue, I am love. I was there long ago, I am here with you always. Do not be fearful. Listen to my words, for they come with great promise, hope, care, and concern."

For one brief instant, Angela glimpsed a figure cloaked in a silver, purple, and gold garment which flowed and danced in the air as if it was being blown about by a gentle wind. She could not make out facial features, yet she felt drawn to the being in some mystical, magical way. And then it was gone.

She almost felt disappointment, but her fatigue took over and, laying her head on the soft down filled pillow, turning on her side, she closed her eyes and in seconds was fast asleep, dreaming the dreams of an innocent child. Wonderful dreams which came from a pure, uncontaminated soul. Dreams she would well remember. Dreams that would affect her future. Dreams of her ultimate destiny.

In the background played a soft melody, so pure in tone words could not describe it. It was the music of absolute harmony and love; the music of life.

JOSHUA REVISITED

The cold tile of the bathroom floor was the first sensation Joshua felt when he regained consciousness. His mind brought back the memories of the unexplainable incident he had just experienced. Gathering the little vigor left in him, he pushed his body upward, pressing both hands on the tiled floor, crouched, and stood up. He shook his head to and fro in an effort to clear his foggy mind and get his wits about him once more. A bit apprehensive, Joshua looked directly into the bathroom mirror, half expecting to be scared out of his wits. This time, reflected back at him was his own ashen face, bewilderment written all over it. As he took in his surroundings, he found no sign whatsoever of anything weird, uncanny, or strange. The white porcelain sink, once defiled with vomit, reptiles, bugs, and bits of assorted other repugnant substances, now stood shiny and clean, not a trace of evidence that anything unusual had ever taken place. He reached for the toothpaste, half afraid of smelling that inexpressible stench finding it smelled only of peppermint. He hesitantly squeezed a dab of the toothpaste onto his fingertip, touching the front of his tongue to the small amount and finding the pleasant all-familiar taste.

Have I dreamt this entire episode? Am I going daft? thought Joshua as he walked cautiously into the bedroom and sneaked a quick glance at the clock set on his bedside table. He noticed it was 10:17 p.m. and that nearly four hours had passed since he had originally entered his bathroom.

Surely Joansie was frantic with worry by this time or, worse yet, quite upset about being stood up, something Joshua would never do. To other women, sure, he'd done it hundreds of times. Made a date with them, and then, after they had willingly given up their bodies to him, they never heard from him again.

Easy women were easy to find. They seemed to be drawn to Joshua as if a giant magnet was attached to his body. He smirked at the memories of these dim-witted souls. Hadn't mother warned them of men such as he? Bet they wished they had listened to mother's advice. He chuckled just thinking about the lot of them.

Joshua wondered if it was too late to give Joansie a call. And what was he to tell her? That he'd gone completely bonkers and was having mental and physical hallucinations? Better to reflect on a suitable excuse for his absence. He was certain he'd come up with the proper explanation; he'd call her tomorrow. Now was the time to get some much needed rest.

Yawning, Joshua stripped down to his boxer shorts, slid under the sheets, pulled both blanket and comforter over his long slender body, and looked forward to losing himself in a good night's sleep. However, for what seemed half the night, he tossed and turned.

He couldn't get the calls and horrific experience out of his mind, and kept reliving every ghastly moment, trying to figure it out. None of it made any sense. Nothing was logical.

Eventually his mind succumbed to his body's needs and he fell into deep slumber, finally, a sleep that allowed him the peace he sought.

***

Music played as he slept, contained in a dream. It was brutal, pounding, harsh throbbing notes that clashed with one another. Drums beat on the off-beat, violins screeched with sour tones, and a baritone voice barked out foul venom-filled verses. Scenes from his life flashed before his eyes amid the dark rhythm. He saw his sister, Beth, begging him for assistance when she had to tell their parents she was pregnant at the age of fifteen. He saw himself chastise her, calling her whore, slut, and telling her he was ashamed she was his sister. How could she bring such shame to their family, and especially to him? Did she know what the kids at school would do now? Did she? His words rang clear as he mimicked the school kids saying "Josh, by gosh, your sister's a tramp. She'll sleep with anyone, given the chance."

Beth shrieked and sobbed, telling Joshua to stop saying such hurtful things about her. She told him she had only been with one boy, Ernie Fox. Josh heard himself answer, "Yeah, sure, like I believe that bunch of hooey, you whore."

Her face turned toward him and he saw the pain, need, and love for him in her eyes. Still, he ordered her out of his room. No one brought shame upon him and got away with it. He didn't care if she was his sister, or how good and kind she had been to him in the past. As far as he was concerned, he now had no sister. Didn't she realize the ridicule and taunts he'd have to endure thanks to her?

That was the exact moment he banished her from his life.

Then the dream scene changed to his parents' bedroom. He saw a fragile old man who resembled his father, lying in the queen-sized bed, constantly coughing, able to come up for breath every few seconds before another round of coughing spasms resumed. A young man entered the room, and Joshua saw it was himself at age twenty-seven. His father ceased the coughing and raised his hand, motioning Joshua near, a smile on his wrinkled lips. The young dream-Joshua stood his ground, drawing no closer to the dying figure in the bed.

"Please son," gasped his father. "I want to hold your hand in mine this one last time. That is all I ask."

"You sicken me, Father. Spend your life chewing nasty smelly tobacco and now you want me to feel sorry that you are dying of cancer. Sorry, but it's not in me. How I figure it, you knew what you were up against when you chewed that foul-smelling junk. Don't expect any sympathy or regrets from me. I have nothing to offer you."

"What about ... love?" the feeble voice said.

"Love? You're concerned about my loving you now? It's a bit late for that, dear Father, isn't it? Can't remember you ever loving me or showing any affection my way, can you?"

His father was silent.

"Didn't think you could come up with an answer. Where were you all my life when I needed you, when I'd come home from school crying my eyes out over being teased and bullied? That's right, you were nowhere in sight. Once, I would have welcomed this show of affection you present me, but not now and not ever. Goodbye, Father."

He watched as his father cried out after him, "No, son, you ... don't ... under ... stand. But the younger Joshua Allan had already left ears' reach, leaving his father to die with the knowledge his son hated his guts.

ROSIE'S PLIGHT

Bright fluorescent light from the bathroom was the first thing Rosie sensed as she regained consciousness. The glare caused her to blink several times. Try as she might, she could not grasp what had just transpired. Nothing about the experience was logical. For a brief moment, Rosie doubted her own recollection, preferring to believe it had been a hallucination or figment of her imagination. She braced herself against the toilet seat lid, pulled up the weight of her shaken body, tossed back the locks of hair from her face, and brushed down the nightgown that had fallen askew on her large frame. With her back to the mirror, Rosie felt unadulterated terror, afraid to turn her head for fear of what the reflection would confirm. Yet, inquisitive, she cautiously rotated her full body toward the oval mirror above the bathroom basin. She could not help but let out a shriek of joy to find her reflection clear of welts and boils.

To her astonishment and amazement the bathroom looked exactly as it had when she first entered it, before evil had taken over, before insanity raised its ugly head. For the first time in her life, Rosie was bewildered, anxious, and apprehensive over something she could not control.

First the DVD, now this. Whatever could it mean? How would she go on? She surely couldn't contact the authorities or tell her friends. They would think her a looney-tune, a stark raving imbecile. Rosie darted to the living room, sat down on the rose-embossed divan, put her head in her hands and cried tears of both dread and relief. The sobs were loud; the tears flowed steadily, taking away any strength left in her body. She wailed and sobbed as a punished child sent to their room, only able to refrain when weariness sent her drifting into a fitful night's sleep. The last thought on her mind was: "Whatever am I going to do?"

***

"Rosie, Rosie, who walks like a snail. Rosie, Rosie, skinny as a rail. Rosie, Rosie, your clothes are thread-bare and given to you by charities who care. Their old second hand junk is all you wear. Rosie, Rosie, with that carrot-topped hair. Rosie, Rosie, trailer trash. Rosie, Rosie, don't come too near, 'cause if you do, your head we'll bash.

She stirred in her sleep, while dark, brooding, angry music entered her mind, drawing forth suppressed memories from long ago. She tried to resist the ear-piercing tones as well as the hateful, horrid memories of the past; still they continued on.

She saw a young red-headed girl of nine, so thin and frail a strong wind could blow her over with one strong puff. The girl wore a dirty, scraggly dress two sizes too large for her tiny frame and had on scuffed black shoes with holes worn in the bottoms. She wore no socks, and shivered in the cold, autumn air. There was hopelessness, need, and desperation in the young girl's large eyes. Fact was this child had never had one day that she did not go to bed hungry for both food and affection. Her parents, both shiftless drunks, left their seven children to do as they pleased. Already her older brother, Jeff, was in the penitentiary for stealing food and money from the local stores. And her sister, Mary, hadn't fared much better since she ran off and eloped with that no good Alvin guy. He put a roof over their head but at the price of Mary never knowing when the next beating would come. All it took was a look he felt wasn't right and then into arguing which always ended with a bruised Mary begging his forgiveness.

By thirteen, Rosie had developed into a beauty. Her once carrot-colored hair had turned a rich auburn. Her skinny body was now full and voluptuous, and those eyes of hers, no man could resist her glance. Add a smile from her pouty mouth and he was hooked. Yet Rosie had no idea of the affect she had on the male gender, nor did she care. Years of sexual abuse from her uncle ruined any chance of a normal male/female relationship for Rosie. He had started the abuse when she was a mere seven years old and it had continued until she was eleven. She'd tried to tell her parents; in their alcoholic stupor, they blamed her for the abuse, said they'd talk to Uncle Steve, but never had done so. The only reason the abuse stopped was he favored little girls and Rosie had grown too mature for his liking. She remembered the first time it happened, all the depraved details. That was when the music started its dark, cynical beat. It grew stronger each day until it surrounded her heart and worked deep into her very soul. She knew that once she was an adult, she'd get them before they got her. Who? Well, all people, of course. No one would penetrate the hold the music had on her, nor did she wish anyone to do so.

A NEW MORNING FOR JOSHUA

After waking and taking a much needed shower, Joshua prepared three eggs over easy, wheat toast with blueberry jam, and diced potatoes with peppers and onions. He poured himself a cup of strongly brewed coffee and added a teaspoon of Irish cream before sitting down to enjoy his breakfast. In minutes, Joshua had consumed every morsel and let out a loud belch. He smacked his lips in satisfaction from a meal greatly desired and enjoyed.

The memories of yesterday's events slowly encompassed his thoughts. How was he to approach Joansie? Perhaps honesty would work in this particular situation; after all, it was Joansie. She would give him reassurance, and that was exactly what he needed today, someone to listen and not judge. Hell, she already knew what he was capable of, those acts that would cause most to feel shame or disgrace. Instead, he felt a sense of pride and smugness. Remorse, guilt, or repentance were not a part of his character or moral fiber. He was a self-made man. One who lived the rat-race, survived and overcame its obstacles. How could he not feel satisfaction from his accomplishments? He was the envy of the masses in this crumb bum little college town. Anybody with an ounce of sense would give his or her right hand to boast the fame, fortune, and power he possessed.

Lighting his first cigarette of the day and inhaling deeply, Joshua made his way to the bedroom. He sat on the edge of the bed, running his fingers through his mass of thick hair, and reached for his personal cell phone. He was geared up to tell Joansie of his strange experiences and apologize for standing her up. He grabbed the phone, opened it, and pushed the number pad, when suddenly he was thrown six feet across the room from an electrical force emitted by his, until now trusty phone, landing on the beige Berber rug.

Dazed and stunned by the shocks that coursed through his body, Joshua quivered as he attempted to stand upright and regain his footing. He stumbled to his bed, using the left corner to recover stability as he pressed his hands against the linen covered mattress and tossed his body onto the bed. Through the murkiness in his brain, he questioned how a small cell phone could cause such a tremendous jolt to his body that it would throw him across the room. Indisputably, this was unlike anything he had ever heard of happening. How was he to explain it? The cell phone provider would have a field day with him. No, he would not set himself up for such ridicule and mockery.

"Wish I had a land-line," thought Joshua. Sullen and shaken, he was apprehensive of touching the cell phone anytime in the foreseeable future.

Perhaps he would simply drop by Joansies' apartment. She would be there, he was sure, as she was not much of an early riser. With this plan in mind, Joshua starting dressing. He chose the dark blue Levi Strauss jeans and a black and white striped cashmere sweater, pulled on his socks, slid his feet into the black Fia athletic shoes at his feet, and rushed to his Corvette. He was ready to escape the surrealistic happenings of the last two days. After sliding into the driver's seat, buckling his seatbelt and turning on the ignition, Joshua sped off to seek the consolation of his dear friend.

Joansies' eyes flickered a bit as she fought to drown out the rapping noise which awakened her from a most magnificent dream. "Oh," she groaned before yelling at the noise, Go away! I'm not out of bed yet. Come back later."

Knowing some encouragement might be needed to rouse Joansie this early in the morning, Joshua yelled through the door, "It's me, Joshua. Joansie, let me in. I must talk with you. It's important! Please, my sunshine, let me in?" Not hearing a reply, Joshua knocked on the door, rapping five more times until he was certain he heard movement coming from the other side of the entrance. He stood back a bit, awaiting the opening of the apartment door.

Abruptly the door swung open to reveal a tousled, disheveled Joansie on the other side. She still looked sexy to him. What a natural beauty she possessed. It was one he believed most women could not achieve without the aid of mascara and face makeup.

"Okay, come on in, Josh, but I'm having some coffee before I do one more thing, understand?"

That was fine with him; he could use another cup or two of java and maybe a jigger of rum to give him the nerve to speak of his latest adventures. "Make mine java and rum, if you don't mind, my lady," said Joshua to the half-asleep half awake Joansie.

"Geez, Josh, it isn't even nine a.m. and you want a drink already," questioned Joansie. Seeing the pleading glance Joshua gave her, she countered with, "Sure, Josh, whatever you want. Now sit down while I make the coffee, and tell me what this is all about."

Joshua took a seat on the yellow and white vinyl vintage '50s chair which was part of a five-piece set Joansie had set up in her kitchen breakfast nook. It wasn't to Joshua's taste. Truth be known, he found the entire set cheap and shabby looking. He'd offered to take it to the local dump numerous times, knowing Joansie would respond, as she always did, with a loud and definite, "No way, Jose." Why she found these old relics things of beauty he'd never understand, but that was Joansie. She loved the old stuff. Her apartment was full of chipped urns and vases, faded and soiled memorabilia from the past century. In fact, her junk took up every spare nook and cranny. Made him dizzy taking in the hundreds of trinkets and knickknacks surrounding him. Good thing he wasn't claustrophobic.

"Why so quiet and sullen," Joansie asked as she slid into the chair across the table, looking straight into his appealing blue eyes, an arched-browed expression of puzzlement on her pretty face.

Joshua, uncharacteristically, hung his face toward the floor, evading Joansies' questioning stare while letting out a long sigh of exasperation, inwardly searching for the correct words to say. Words that he feared, yet words he had to express to someone, and soon. He needed that drink bad.

"How long before that java is ready? Hell, forget the java, how about that rum? I'll take it straight, and I'll take it right now."

Joansie, without hesitation, rose from her chair, took out a small four-ounce drinking glass, located the rum in her small liquor cabinet and proceeded to pour the dark liquid into the glass, filling it to the brim before she handed it to Joshua. In one swift movement he gulped down the entire contents, feeling the burning sensation run down his throat as a flush of heat slowly generated through his body, relaxing him and giving him the courage he so desperately sought.

The coffee now ready, Joansie poured herself a large cupful, added French vanilla creamer, and sat down across from her friend once again. She sipped her coffee, pleased with the taste the vanilla added to the brew. Now quite alert and prepared to hear what news was having such a stranglehold on Joshua, she ran her finger over the rim of her large cup, turned toward him, and in a half whisper said, "Okay, sweetums, your turn. I'm all ears."

"Joans, you've know me for years. You know that I base truth on facts, right?"

Joansie nodded her head in total agreement.

"Well, what I am about to tell you may be difficult to comprehend and even more difficult to believe. I assure you, it is real, it is a fact, and it has shaken my world a bit. You must promise me you will never, ever repeat what I am about to say to you. This is a friendship breaker, understand? Do you agree to keep this only between the two of us," asked Joshua.

With a chuckle, Joansie replied "Of course, Josh, it goes without saying. Your secret is safe with me. You know that."

Finding the nerve to continue, Joshua began his tale, recounting the strange occurrences while Joansie listened in amazement, disbelief, and grave concern for her friend's sanity. She'd never known Joshua to be anything but honest with her, yet all she could say to him after hearing the story of last night's events was, "Josh, I don't know what to say to you. You don't show up to meet me, turn up on my doorstep this morning with tales that are so farfetched no person in their right mind would take them seriously. But you expect me to believe you." Gently placing her right hand on top of his and giving it a subtle pat, Joansie peered into the sky-blue eyes of her long-time friend and said, "Let me ask you this: if the tables were turned, would you believe me? Would you not question my senses or my reasoning?"

Joshua, a bit unnerved and embarrassed, simply stared back, unable to find the words she would understand. Knowing everything he had spoken was the truth while knowing it to be unbelievable, even to such a close friend as Joansie, he finally responded, "I shouldn't have come here. I realize I sound like a lunatic. How am I to expect anyone, even you, to accept my words as truth? All I'm able to tell you is what happened. I don't understand any of it myself, but I swear to you these events took place. I also guarantee I'm not a madman. What I am, Joans, is scared out of my wits. Being humble is not one of my strong points, but today, in front of you, I am the most humble man in the world. All I ask of you is to make no judgment at this time. Simply be my friend, Joans. Even if you can't believe these things happened, believe that they are my reality."

Joansie rose and walked around the table, unable to contain the tears of compassion she felt for her dear friend. Standing behind Joshua as he sat, she put her arms around his shoulders and chest, giving him the biggest hug of comfort she could muster. Placing her chin on his head, Joansie said, "I don't know what is going on but I vow to you that I'm here anytime you need me. My suggestion to you right now is that you head on home, take a couple of my Valium, get some rest, and call me when you wake up. Or if you don't want to be alone, you can stay here with me for as long as you wish, Josh. It's up to you. The one thing I do know is you have to stop worrying about this. It was probably some prankster or some guy who thinks you did him wrong rigging up your phone and putting some chemical into your toothpaste. Doubt it will happen again, but, Josh, if you want to go to the police with this, I'll stand behind you. I'll verify you are as sane as sane can be. Just let me know, okay?"

Joshua turned his body to the left, grabbed Joansie's arms and swept her onto his lap. Nuzzling her, he said, "Babe, no way am I going to the cops with this. I don't need the publicity or want to be the butt of their jokes. I will take you up on those Valiums, though. Promise I'll go straight home, take a snooze, and ring you up this evening. You're probably right about this being someone who lost a bundle from investment advice I gave him. Christ, it could be any number of people with today's market as it is." Joshua placed his forefinger under Joansie's chin, wiped the stray tears from her face, and in an authoritve voice said, "Let's see a smile on that beautiful mug of yours. I didn't come over to bum you out and ruin your day." Joansie reacted by placing a small quick kiss on Joshua's lips, then hopped up from his lap and headed to the bedroom to retrieve the much-needed Valium. Joshua rose as she re-entered the room, took the pills from her hand, placed them in his wallet, gave Joansie a firm pat on the rear, along with a promise to call her the moment he woke up. She led him to the door, opened it and blew him a small kiss when he glanced her way before entering the open elevator.

Joshua was glad he had decided to confide in Joansie. She was perhaps the only person who understood him and accepted his idiosyncrasies. The rum worked its magic. He was actually humming as he walked toward his bright red car, looking forward to arriving home, ingesting the Valium that would give his over-active mind the rest it dearly needed. Josh opened the car door, fit his long body into the driver's seat, secured the safety belt, and started the engine. He pulled a cigarette out of the box, lit it, enjoying the calm it gave him as he inhaled and let out a long puff of smoke. He checked the rearview and driver's side mirrors for clearance and pulled out into the roadway, singing to the 70s rock music blasting from the radio, and thinking, "This isn't such a bad day, after all".

INSIDE EUCLID'S HEAD

"Damn it to hell," Euclid cried out as he nicked his left thumb with the knife. He brought the digit to his mouth and sucked the blood that oozed from the wound. Hadn't he told Johnny to be careful of the razor-sharp blade? Now he was the one who wasn't concentrating. Ah, the irony of it all, perhaps the irony of life.

Euclid rose from the porch bench and went inside in search of a Band-Aid. Familiar voices buzzed in his head. They were coming frequently, but always catching him by surprise. Why choose him? He was a good, church going man who lived a simple life. He'd always come to the aid of others in their time of need, and now questioned whether he should speak to Harry or the pastor about what was taking hold of him. How could he, though? Never before had he felt such shame. A force greater than he had taken firm hold of both body and mind. He'd attempted to fight the force with all his might. It was useless. He was weak in comparison and continued to do as he was instructed. The voices coached, whispering sweet melodic words into his ears, words that belied the depravity of the actions insisted upon.

As he reached into the medicine cabinet, fumbling to locate the box of Band-Aids, a voice said to him, "Why do you fight me? Have I not promised you I will take care of you? Why do you doubt me? Have I not vowed to be by your side, to walk with you and give you strength? Euclid, all that I ask of you is necessary. All that I say to you is truth."

Euclid placed his large hands over his ears in an effort to stop the voice and cried out, "Why me? I am no one special. For what reason do ya seek me out among all the rest? Jus' leave me to myself! I don't understand. Please, I don't wanna hear no more. I did what you told me. Don't ask me to do anything else!"

He listened, expecting to hear the voice again. Instead, there was silence.

And the visions, oh, yes, the visions. Creeping into his mind when he was in bed, not quite asleep but not quite awake, either. *She* would come to him and sit by his side, looking as she had when they were first married. So beautiful and peaceful, dressed in a white flowing gown, ribbons of gold and silver adorning her black hair. Not at all as she appeared when the ravishment of cancer took its toll on her fragile body and mind.

Gina, his wife, come to comfort old Euclid. How he yearned to feel the touch of her hand upon his face, the warmth and softness of her body against his. He missed her so. She would sit upon the corner of the bed and he would hear her words in his head. The softness of her voice entered his mind, projected with a tone of concern, *Do not fear, my love. You are a special man. This, I have known all my life, my dear Euclid. You have a special mission to accomplish. It is of the utmost importance, my sweet. Listen to the wind and what it whispers in your ear. Heed the signs and follow the urges that will propel you to take action. What seems senseless and irrational holds purpose. The reason is not for you to understand. Euclid, your soul is pure, untainted by the temptations of life, and that is why you must hold no fear of what is happening to you, nor question the actions you take. I am here by your side. I will always be near to you. Keep your faith dear to you; follow your heart and your conscience for they will not lead you astray.*

Then she would be gone.

She had appeared to him several times. He wanted to believe it was really her. Sure looked just like her when she was young. He was so forlorn and lost since her passing. It was all becoming too much for him to figure out. He was supposed to follow Gina and the voices without question, was he?

Then there was that other mental picture. The one when he'd seen two women. One was young, maybe in her mid twenties or so. She sure was pretty and had a real nice smile. Couldn't figure out what she wanted from him. She'd gaze into his face with an understanding, loving look. Didn't say nothing at all; just stared at him. And this other lady, well, she was probably middle aged and she wore a nurse's uniform. Or, at least, it looked like a nurse's uniform. Anyways, she'd gaze at him with what he could only think of as a 'caretaker' look, the look of someone taking care of a sick person. Just can't figure any of this out an' it's drivin' me bonkers, thought Euclid as he wrapped the Band-Aid around the large cut on his finger.

As he stood wrapping his finger, the voice whispered to him, "You have done well. You will find the answers you seek. I am with you always. Fear not the unknown. Believe in goodness, grace, and love."

Then, complete silence.

No more! I can't take this one more second," shouted Euclid Hannigan.

A sob caught in his throat as he thought of what he had become. He *couldn't* take it any longer, those voices telling him to be patient, and Gina saying to follow their instructions. No, it wasn't right. What was he to believe? Where was he to turn for comfort? Who would understand what he had done? It suddenly became apparent to him the step he must take to end it all. It was clear, what he had to do – and he knew he had to do it quick before he lost his nerve.

Euclid slowly walked toward the garage, opened the door, shuffling his feet as he sought the long cardboard box leaning against the rear wall. Resolve and intention were the only emotions Euclid possessed as he cut through the cardboard and pulled out the shiny new rifle. He glowed with the excitement of Christmas morning, positive it was the path he must follow.

AT THE FRANKS'

As promised, Angela cooked pancakes; plain for Alexis and blueberry for Alicia and Monty. What an appetite this brood of hers had. They ate every single pancake, and she had prepared over two dozen of them.

Monty patted his full belly, let out a small belch and said, "Ang, that was wonderful. Think I may have to make another notch in my belts if you keep cooking meals like this for me."

"Monty Frank, say excuse me. Where are your manners? What type of example are you setting for the girls?" replied Angela.

"But, hon, it's your fault. If you weren't such a great cook, I wouldn't eat so much," said Monty as he gave Angela a quick wink.

"Oh, yeah, blame it on me." She laughed. "I believe you and the twins require a brisk hike around the neighborhood to walk off that heavy breakfast. How's that sound?"

Monty winced at the thought of exerting himself, especially on a full stomach. He glanced at his wife and knew there was no getting around this walk. She was determined to keep her family as fit as possible. She'd been trying for years to get him on a regular exercise routine, amidst his objections.

Before he was able to protest any further, Angela called "Come on Alicia, Alexis. Your dad wants to take you for a walk."

With the energy and zest for adventure only young children possess, the twins raced toward Monty.

"Can we stop at the park and go on the swings, Daddy?" This from Alexis. Alicia took hold of both of Monty's hands, stretched his arms out and pulled him in the direction of the front door.

"Whoa, girls, hold on. Daddy needs to get dressed first. Or do you want to be seen with your old dad in his jammies?"

The girls squealed with laughter, picturing their father out in front of everybody in his pajamas.

"Course not, Daddy," said Alicia, adding, "Can we take Gumption with us, too? He wants to go to the park with us."

"All right, you two, you talked me into it. Yes, bring Gumption along. Think you both need to get out of your nightgowns, brush your teeth, and comb those mops of hair, don't you? Or were you both planning on wearing your jammies, too?" teased Monty, looking back at the twins as he went up the stairs toward his bedroom.

Turning her attention toward her sister, Alexis stated, "No way am I wearing my jammies outside."

"Me either," Alicia agreed, as they scurried off to get ready.

Within minutes, they were dressed and out the door, Gumption in tow.

Angela waved goodbye through the kitchen window, watching her family head toward the park. She was finishing loading the dishwasher when Monty's cell phone rang. "Oh, geez," she thought, "what if something happens. He forgot to take his phone."

Not taking his phone was something she couldn't ever remember Monty doing. He always took it with him, no matter what. Must be slipping, Angela chuckled to herself. She picked up the phone and answered, "Hello?"

A clearly angry male voice asked, "Is this Monty Frank's phone?"

"Yes, it is," Angela replied, "He's out right now, may I help you?"

"You tell him I better get a call back, and soon. I've left him seven messages since yesterday. I need to talk to him, it's important. When will he be back?"

A bit unnerved by the intensity in the caller's voice, Angela said, "I'm sorry, Mr.?"

"Bracken. Robert Bracken," the caller said. "I expect a call today. You tell him that."

Angela replied, "Yes, Mr. Bracken, I will see that my husband gets your message. I'm sure he has been very busy and had full intentions of contacting you. I'm sorry for any inconvenience."

"That's all right. Just be sure he gets my message. Thank you," said Bob Bracken.

"You're quite welcome," Angela replied and clicked off the phone.

She poured herself a cup of green tea, added some honey, and sat down at the kitchen table, wondering why this Bracken person was so annoyed. Monty didn't talk much about his work, preferring to keep it separate from his family life. From what Angela understood, he was doing something to help people in financial crunches. He'd told her hundreds of times how he would get a family back on their feet, setting up payment plans that they could afford. She thought he was helping others, but Robert Bracken sure didn't sound like he was pleased with the assistance given him. Monty took care of all their finances, always had. Angela didn't have the experience or desire to be involved in money matters.

Since their marriage, she'd concentrated on attending school, earning her degree, more than happy to let Monty take care of that end of the household responsibilities. She never thought to question his profession; it occurred to her that it might be time she found out what, exactly, his job consisted of. Knowing her family would be back within a couple of hours, Angela put the matter aside; she'd deal with it once Monty returned.

Abruptly, a vision appeared in Angela's mind's eye. She saw a man's blurred figure, his back to her. He was surrounded in a black aura, and he was laughing wickedly. The laughter soon turned into massive sobs of pain and grief, then back to evil sounding chortles. Slowly he turned his face toward her. It gradually grew less blurry until she could make out his features.

"Dear God, no," she cried out, shutting her eyes. Angela pounded her head with her fists in an effort to end this vision, to get it out of her mind. As it faded away, she buried her face in her arms, shuddering as one single tear trailed down her frowning face.

Although it seemed an eternity to her, Monty and the girls arrived home. All three sensed something amiss when Angela did not greet them with her usual cheery hello.

"Hi, hon. You okay," asked Monty as he shooed the twins into the living room to watch some mid-morning cartoons. Angela could not bring herself to answer. She was unable to find the right words and wondered if this was the right time, anyway. She didn't want to say something she might later regret.

"Come on, Ang, I can tell something is eating at you. What happened? Are you okay?" continued Monty. He approached her and put his hand on her shoulder in an effort to show comfort.

After a moment, Angela lifted her face, turned and looked directly into Monty's eyes. Conflict was written all over her face, a face seeking answers, a face never before seen by Monty. Steadying herself against the kitchen sink, she answered in a faint whisper, "Monty, we have to talk. A man called today when you were gone. His name is Robert Bracken and he said you have been ignoring his phone calls. He sounded very annoyed and very persistent. His number is in your cell phone. I want you to call him back. I promised him you would."

"Ang, is that what's bothering you? A client calling me has you this upset?" Brushing it off, Monty said, "I'm dealing with people's money, their lives. Surely one of them will become upset every once in a while. It's expected."

Angela walked to the other side of the kitchen, turned around and stared at Monty. She was going to find out how his business worked. She'd inquired before, but hadn't been really that interested. After the vision she'd seen, she was more than interested. She was intent on getting answers.

"Monty, tell me, what do you do for these people who are in need? How do you help them? I want the truth."

Monty hung his head, a bit sheepishly, Angela thought. Looking toward the floor, he said, "You and the girls are the most important thing in the world to me. You know that, don't you?"

"Of course," Angela replied.

"Well, Ang, I do help people, along with helping us. The way it works is I get their creditors to agree to a lower interest rate, which means they have less to pay back to them. Along with that, I get twenty-five percent of their total debt amount. It pays for me dealing with the creditors and assisting them during the payback period."

"Monty!" Angela gasped. "Twenty-five percent is too much money to charge these unfortunate people. I had no idea you did this. How can you justify such an absorbent amount of money? These people who are already in desperate straits are depending on you to help them, not send them even deeper in debt. So, do you help them with their credit rating? I mean, you must be giving them something of value to charge so much, aren't you?"

Monty walked to the kitchen table, pounded his fist against it, shaking the teacup and saucer she'd left there. A look of absolute rage distorted his features. His face beet red, he turned to her, lips curled upward and shouted,

"So you think you're so holier than thou, do you? Standing there feeling such sorrow for 'these people'. They put themselves in the predicaments they are in; not me, not you. If I wasn't doing this, there are hundreds of other guys they'd get the same deal from, or worse. They'd make a deal with one of them, so why shouldn't it be me? The time is right with the economy in such poor shape, and I have to take advantage of it while it lasts. So they're suckered into it. So what? I'm not doing anything illegal. And you sure haven't complained about the fancy house, clothing, and jewelry this money allows us to buy, have you? We're winners, Ang, not losers like those bunch of saps. Why you even waste your time worrying about them is beyond me. Our family is all that matters. Now I don't want to hear one more word about this. It certainly never bothered you before, why the concern now? Did that guy threaten you? I'll kill the asshole, I swear, before I let anyone harm my family."

Angela backed away from her husband, the man she thought she knew all these years, the man she believed had a heart of gold, the man who now seemed a complete stranger. Quietly she said, "Calm down. No, Mr. Bracken did not threaten me. He simply wanted you to answer his calls. He seemed desperate. And, Monty, don't you ever shout at me like this again. I don't even know you anymore. You've been such a wonderful, loving and truly caring husband and father, I would never have guessed you were so callous and cold-hearted toward the rest of the world. You've known all along how I feel about helping others. You told me you felt the same way. How could you lie to me about this, knowing how important it is to me? Monty, I married you thinking you had a beautiful soul and now I find out how much hatred and contempt you have for the unfortunate. What do you expect me to say? I love the man I thought you were, not the man standing before me today. I don't know what to think anymore."

So, Monty thought to himself, I've been found out. All these years hiding this side of me from my dear, sweet Angela, hoping she'd never uncover my secret thoughts. That damned Bracken! Hell, no, I'm not calling him back, not after this episode.

Monty turned toward his wife and said, "I love you today as much as

I've ever loved you. I'd kill for my family. Please, Ang, don't let this ruin our marriage or ruin our family. I'll do anything to make it better. "

At that moment, the girls appeared in the doorway.

Alicia cried out, "Stop it! Please don't argue with each other. We'll be good, won't we, Alexis? We promise. Just stop fighting." Tears filled the twins' eyes as they searched their parents' faces, seeking a smile and reassurance that all was again right in their world.

Angela rushed over to the girls, took them in her arms, patted them on the head and said "My angels, you have done nothing wrong. Daddy and Mommy were only talking. Guess we got a little too enthusiastic with our opinions. It's okay, don't worry your little heads over this. It's nothing."

She kissed them on the forehead, wiped the tears from their faces and held her arm out, motioning for Monty to join her and the girls. Without hesitation, Monty wrapped his arms around them. The family hugged each other in a powerful grip, clinging together to restore the calm, to take away the fear.

What Angela could not tell Monty about was her vision. That evil man, that terrible laughter, the look in his eyes when he turned his face toward her, the features so clear – the face of her husband. The face of Monty Frank.

WORKING FOR A LIVING

The alarm call went off for the second time from room 417-A. Karman pushed the off button, rose from her seat at the nursing station desk and walked down the hall to see what Mr. Carson needed. She entered his room and went to his bed.

"Joseph, how on earth did you manage to wrap this sheet around your neck? What are you trying to do, commit hari-kari?

"No sirree Bob, I'm not, ma'am. That's why I pushed this button you gave me here. I don't know how this blanket made its way up to my neck. I tell you, it's alive. Was pulling the darn thing up to get warm and it wrapped itself around me."

Karman carefully unraveled the loosely wrapped blanket from her patient's neck.

"Now, Mr. Carson, how many times have I explained that a blanket is an inanimate object and cannot move on its own power?"

"This one did. You have to believe me. It's the wrong color. Please, give me a new blanket. A green one because the green ones like me and won't hurt me. Those white ones are the worst and you keep bringing them back to me."

Joseph Carson, dressed in a flimsy faded blue hospital gown, huffed, then walked to the opposite side of his room and lowered his lanky body into the brown fake-leather chair. Karman saw the fear etched in his face. The doctor had instructed them to use reason with Joseph. It was not working. He'd been here for four days and the terror of the white blankets was intensifying. All she could do now was provide understanding. Logic certainly was not the cure-all for this patient's phobia.

"Tell you what, Joseph. I'll take away the white blankets." She gathered them into her arms saying, "See, I have them right here. Nothing is going to harm you."

Shifting the blankets to one side, Karman pulled out a long, soft green robe from her patients' closet and dangled it in his direction.

Joseph's eyes brightened and his body, once tense, relaxed against the chair.

"You put on this robe your family brought you, okay?" Karman stated as she tossed the robe in Joseph's direction. Reflexively, he caught it mid-flight.

"Yes, ma'am, I will," he answered in a feeble voice.

"I'm going to stand here until you get up out of that chair and slip your robe on. Can't have you running around half naked, now, can we?"

Joseph rose, slipped into the robe and asked, "Will you be bringing me a green blanket?

"I'll talk to the doctor and see what he has to say. He's scheduled to stop by this morning, so we'll have him check in on you, okay?"

"That would be great, ma'am. Thanks."

Karman closed and locked the door as she left but kept the square observation window open.

Her heart went out to these patients. Joseph was one of the more fortunate. Except for a fear of certain colors, he was as normal as they came. She felt with the proper counseling the cause of his fear would become evident. Then he'd be able to face it and begin healing his damaged mind.

Not so with the bi-polars and schizophrenics who faced a life-long battle. She saw too many give up hope, medication, and psychiatric assistance, their worlds becoming ones of fantasy, delirium, mania, and frenzy. Some took their lives to find release. Others delved deeper into their own reality, allowing it to take hold of their minds until it became their only reality.

Worse, hundreds roamed the streets, alone, hungry, and desperate. They were lost souls, these oddities of civilization, doomed to live a clandestine life within the spaces of their minds.

Before Karman could react, Greta Hooten entered the hallway, squatted, and urinated on the freshly washed white tiled floor.

I can see what kind of day I'm in for, thought Karman.

It would prove to be a doozy.

EVERYTHING'S NOT ROSIE

The blare of the television woke Rosie. Some commentator was babbling about the state of the economy again, blaming Washington, Wall Street, and the banks. T'was the same old song that had been playing for too long. For a moment Rosie felt quite normal, stretching her arms and body as she did every morning before rising.

The sun streamed into her living room, filling it with beams of yellow, purple and blue light. Rosie basked in the moment, enjoying the warmth of the sun and the promise of a new day dawning. Gaining awareness, memories of the day before crept into her mind, sending chills down her spine. Shaking it off, she picked up the remote and clicked off the blaring television. Reflecting on the odd events she had experienced last night, Rosie considered phoning her friend, Rita Ashland. She thought about it another moment and decided silence would best serve. No one in their right mind would believe what took place; even she now doubted the entire episode. Logic told her it could have been her imagination or a daydream of sorts. Yet she knew what had taken place. It was Saturday and the beginning of the weekend. She had much to do around the house and garden, not to mention the Richter's Open House scheduled for Sunday.

"No, old Rosie," she reflected, "don't allow this silliness to destroy your life. Time to get up at 'em."

Cautiously, Rosie entered her bathroom, half expecting to see proof of the eerie occurrence, but there was no evidence that anything out of the ordinary had taken place. The bathroom was 'slick as whistle': a shiny, radiantly clean toilet, basin, floor, and walls. There was not one bit of evidence to verify her ordeal. She couldn't reason it out. It made no sense. There was nothing logical about any of it. All she could do, she figured, was put the entire episode behind her. After all, she was a prominent realtor in this area. Letting the cat out of the bag, talking about what she believed she'd experienced, would only bring ridicule and shame to her name.

Rosie guardedly turned on the faucet and stared straight ahead into the mirror above the basin. Her reflection – nothing else – stared back at her. Relief and calmness replaced apprehension and anxiety. She told herself the worst was over and only good things were to come.

After washing her face, brushing her teeth, and combing back her long hair, Rosie padded off to the kitchen set to prepare the morning coffee. Once again content, life back to normal, she started to hum.

As she lifted her arm to pour the water into the coffee maker, a rash on the front of her arm caught her eye. She stopped pouring and set the pot upon the kitchen counter, then put on her glasses to take a much closer look. She had never seen anything like it before. It wasn't a rash, she discovered. It was her skin, except now there was a scaly hard surface where it had once been smooth and soft. The area it covered was approximately three inches long and maybe an inch and a half wide. It didn't itch or feel irritated at all. But the scaliness and color, a greenish-brown, was a bit off-putting.

"Probably some leftover reaction to those welts and boils," she told herself. "I'll put on some cream and cover it up with a bandage. It'll go away in a day or so, I suppose."

Rosie picked up the coffee pot and proceeded to finish pouring the water into the tank of the coffee maker, not giving the change in her skin another thought. If she had further inspected her body, she would have found the same distinct skin change on her inner thighs, backs of her knees, down her spine, and under her arms.

Gracie Honesetter jolted up from her seat and ran to the window to see where in carnation that long, loud, piercing scream had come from. Sounded just as if it had come from Rosie Richards' place. She thought about going over to see if Rosie was all right but was interrupted by the ring of her phone. Soon Gracie was preoccupied in a two hour conversation with her daughter who lived in St. Petersburg, Florida, all thoughts of that scream or Rosie completely forgotten.

PART II

KARMA'S GONNA GET YOU IF YOU DON'T WATCH OUT

Deep within, so far inside,
Lays the truth we cannot hide.
Beneath the outer surface shown,
to those familiar or unknown.

Come take a peek.
A moment's glance

See feelings real,
Join in the dance.

-Monica Brinkman, 2009

SAY IT AIN'T SO, EUCLID

"I've gone mad, cain't fight no more. Time to do what I knows is right," Euclid sing-sang to himself as he set the rifle he'd carried in his right hand down on the concrete floor of his garage. He scooted a long wooden bar stool over to within reach, picked up the weapon and sat down. After checking to see if the rifle was loaded, he pulled a bullet from his pocket, set it inside the rifle chamber, clicked it closed, steadied the rifle on the floor and held it under his chin.

"Gina, forgive me. I just can't take it no more," he said, looking toward the ceiling.

He shut his eyes and pulled the trigger, ready to face the world beyond the curtain of life. Hearing the click of the rifle, he braced himself, but ... nothing happened. Perhaps I didn't load 'er right, he thought as he examined the contents of the chamber. Euclid's eyes doubled in size as he peered into the now empty chamber. *What the heck is goin on here? I know I just loaded this thing. This can't be.*

Euclid crouched on one knee, looked toward the ceiling, and said with conviction, "Can't you see I'm just an old man, one who's bone-weary tired of this life?" He stood, held his arms out and continued to look upward, now shouting, "Voices, can ya hear me? I'm not a strong man, not without my Gina, not without my work. I have no life anymore. You must see that each day brings such hopelessness and grief. I've had enough of it all. I listened to ya. I did the things ya wanted me to do and all ya can tell me is to be patient." Euclid whirled around, looking at the garage walls, speaking to the air, hoping whatever was invading his mind would hear him. He lowered his eyes and brushed away a tiny tear that had trickled down his face. In a soft, loving voice, he again turned his eyes upward asking, "Gina, are you there? Please understand, sweetie. I just can't go on this way. I likes people. I don't wanna hurt nobody no more. Those calls I made, the DVD, the e-mails I sent, they aren't things I shoulda done. Ya understand, don't ya, Gina, what I have to do and why? This force is tougher than your Euclid."

A rage much stronger than he'd ever felt flooded him. He clenched his fists to his side, then raised one hand, pointed his finger upward and bellowed, "So voice, ya think you're so smart ya can stop ole Euclid, huh? I got other ways to take care of this, to end it all."

He chuckled a bit, certain nothing would get in his way, nothing would prevent the completion of his mission. For a second Euclid waivered as he heard her saying to him, "No, my husband, you must not carry through with this. You don't understand. I can't tell you what will come to pass. You must have faith; you must believe."

Truth was he didn't know what to believe anymore. He dismissed the words as madness, craziness he would no longer endure. "It's gotta be ... must be free," he whispered, knowing his course of action was best.

Euclid tossed the rifle onto the wooden shelf he made years ago and started rummaging through the items piled in the corner of his garage. Finding what he was looking for, he climbed up on the bar stool and flung the thick hemp rope over a wooden ceiling beam. He secured the rope by tying it tightly, then tugged on it to be sure it would hold. After he made a slipknot, Euclid put his head through it and pulled it tight to his neck. "Can't stop me, don't ye try. Not when I'm about to die," he chuckled.

In one quick move, he jumped off the barstool, intent on carrying out his suicide. Pain seared through his body as he hit the hard concrete floor. His left leg jutted out from his body at a peculiar angle, and he lay in shock as he looked up to see the heavy rope clearly cut in two, one piece still around his neck, the other dangling from the beam. As pain overtook him, Euclid fell into unconsciousness, but not before thinking, "This can't be. It's impossible."

Jimmy, anxious to see his friend, hurried up the steps of Euclid's porch and knocked on the door. Mr. Hannigan had promised to give him more whittling lessons today and he was eager to get started. Not getting an answer, Jimmy knocked louder. Still no one appeared to let him in. Shucks, Jimmy thought, I walked all this way an' now he's not even home." Disappointed, Jimmy went down the porch stairs, passing the garage as he left for home.

"What's that," Jimmy wondered as he heard what sounded like a hurt animal.

He listened more intently. There it was again. It sounded like it came from the garage. Jimmy got on his tiptoes and looked through the garage door glass. His heart raced as he saw his friend Mr. Hannigan sprawled across the garage floor, his leg bent funny. Jimmy tried to get the garage door open, but it was locked. He raced back up the porch, opened the unlocked front door and ran into the garage via the kitchen to come to his friend's aid.

"Mr. Hannigan, Mr. Hannigan, you all right," Jimmy questioned, shaking his friend's shoulder to see if he was alive.

Euclid opened his eyes and whispered, "Jimmy, think my leg's broken. I can't get up." With concern, Jimmy announced, "I'm gonna go get Ma and Pa. They'll take care of ya, Mr. Hannigan. Don't worry. I'll be right back."

Jimmy couldn't help notice the rope still hanging around Mr. Hannigan's neck. He didn't want to think about that right now. All he wanted to think about was getting help to his friend as soon as possible. Running at a speed he didn't know he possessed, Jimmy bounded through the door into the living room. Luckily, his pa was watching TV.

"Pa, it's Mr. Hannigan. He's hurt real bad. He's lying on the floor in his garage. Think his leg's broke. He looks something awful," reported Jimmy.

Without hesitation, Mr. Johansen picked up the phone and called 911. Quickly, help was on the way.

JOSHUA FEELS THE FORCE OF THE WHEEL

Still humming in good humor, Joshua Allen pulled into his driveway, parked the 'Vette in the garage, opened his door and exited the vehicle. The car's alarm blared just as he reached for the handle of the door that led into his home. He turned back to find out why, and slid to the floor, feeling more horrified than he had ever felt in his life. The sound ceased as he watched the paint on the passenger side door of his car bubble and form letters – one by one – effervescing, moving as if the paint was a living, breathing creature, embossing the letters until they spelled out: You've got your money. You've got your fame. You've got your future of hurt and pain.

Joshua ran to the car, rubbed his hands swiftly over the passenger side door in an effort to erase the message. The paint began pulsing in a heartbeat rhythm, changing the letters into throbbing, illuminated blues, yellows, purples, and greens. He drew his hands away from heat so intense it burned his palms and fingertips.

"Oh, my God," Joshua blubbered, staring at his red hands in utter disbelief. His body shook in fear and terror.

When he found the courage to look up, his vehicle stood before him with no sign of damage and no trace of letters or words. The paint was glistening and smooth. Joshua paced back and forth. He inspected every inch of his vehicle. He needed to know he wasn't going crazy, that what he'd just seen had really happened. He could swear he heard maniacal laughter and a faint voice repeating that damned message over and over again. Seeking solace, he fled to the safety of his home.

For what felt like hours, Joshua stood in his kitchen shaking and trembling from head to toe, unable to stop. Tears ran down his face, falling onto the Italian tiled floor. He clutched his fists and grabbed at the ends of his black hair, then let out a long horrified scream. Gobs of his thick, raven hair stuck to his hands. He fell to his knees, then curled into a fetal position on the floor.

While he sobbed in fear and anguish, thoughts filtered into his foggy mind: pictures from his past. He tried to repress the painful memories, but they wouldn't stop. Scenes of himself walking up to his sister's house and knocking on the front door. When there was no answer, he tried the knob; it turned and he entered her living room. He called out her name, "Beth." Again, "Beth". Hearing no reply, the younger Joshua ran up the stairs and into the master bedroom. "Oh, God, no," he bellowed. At the foot of her bed lay his sister, blood seeping from the deep cuts in each wrist, her eyes open in death. He vowed from that day forward, never to allow himself to feel anything for anyone. And God, well, He certainly didn't exist or, if He did, He didn't favor Joshua Allan, for sure.

The dark music flowed; he became cold, hard-hearted. Never again would he hear the universal music of light and love; instead, his soul filled with envy, greed, lust, and vanity.

***

Joshua Allen, once so proud, lay on his expensive kitchen floor blubbering mindlessly, calling for his mommy, calling to anyone or anything that could save his sanity.

HI HO, INTO THE
PSYCH WARD WE GO

His eyes opening to unfamiliar surroundings, Euclid scanned the small white room. His first instinct was to jump up, an action he discovered was impossible as he was bound securely to the hospital bed. Upon further inspection, Euclid saw his leg was in a cast and held in place by some sort of swing contraption. Though his memory was a bit vague, he remembered lying on the garage floor, unable to rise, when someone had lifted him onto a stretcher, put him in an ambulance and stuck a needle in his arm. That was the last thing he recalled. So, he was in the hospital, was he?

A jolt of pain seared through his broken leg. Involuntarily, Euclid let out a feeble cry of pain. Beads of perspiration formed on his forehead as he fumbled for the call button. He needed relief and he needed it now.

As though she was reading his mind, a nurse appeared in his doorway. For an instant, their eyes locked. Well, hell's bells, thought Euclid. This woman looked familiar. Same thick frizzy hair, large eyes framed by thick lenses, and pleasantly plump body shape as he had seen in his vision. He noticed she wore a white name tag pinned to the upper left breast of her blue uniform. Karman. *Ah, so Karman was her name.*

"Mr. Hannigan, how are you this morning," asked the woman.

"Could be better, ma'am. My leg hurts somethin' fierce," answered Euclid weakly.

Karman checked her patient's chart for the prescribed dosage of pain medication. "I'll be right back with something that will fix you up."

"Thank you kindly, ma'am."

Euclid's eyes followed the nurse as she exited the room. Where had he seen her before? He grimaced as another jolt of pain went through his leg, derailing all thought. He sure wished she would hurry up with that medicine.

On cue, the nurse entered the room and injected the morphine into the tube feeding into Euclid's arm.

"Now lie back and relax, you'll start feeling relief in a few minutes."

"'Preciate it. I ain't one to complain, but it hurts like Hades."

Euclid noticed his nurse was giving him a most peculiar look. Puzzlement was written on her face.

"Anything wrong, ma'am," he asked

"No, Mr. Hannigan. Just you remind me of someone and I'm trying to figure out whom."

"Well, I'll be darned. I've been sittin' here tryin' to figure out the same thing about you, Ms.?"

"Shelton, but you can call me Karman."

" And you can call me Euclid, Ms. Karman. I swear old Euclid has seen ya before, just can't figure out where."

Their eyes locked. As Euclid gazed into Karman's large brown eyes, feelings long suppressed surfaced. He felt a blanket of love and passion wrap around him as desire churned within his body. Karman trembled as sparks of electrifying ardor passed through her body.

A young man carrying a tray of food entered the room, breaking the spell. Karman turned her head away for a second, brushed off a bit of imaginary lint from her collar, turned back toward Euclid, and said, "Mr. Hannigan, you enjoy your meal, and ring that call button should you require anything further. Right now, the best medicine is nourishment and rest. I suspect the doctor will be coming around after lunch to see how you're doing. Be prepared to answer some questions. And I advise you to answer them honestly. We're here to get you well, Euclid."

Euclid nodded, his eyes a bit heavy as the medication took effect.

With a wave of her hand, Karman left him to enjoy his meal. This was one patient she was intent to watch closely. There was something special about him. Her curiosity aroused, she looked forward to helping him cope with the demons that had pushed him into such a state that he would resort to suicide.

Echoing her thoughts, she heard a voice in her ear state, "Tend to this man, Karman. His healing lies within your hands and deep within your heart."

Karman could not help but smile in anticipation of what now lay before her. Her heart beat fast with excitement and exhilaration. She now had reason and purpose beyond anything she had known in her life.

Yes, her time had come. Of this, she was sure.

A NEW PATIENT
FOR ANGELA

It was late in the morning when Angela heard of the new admission to the Psych Unit at the hospital. A man who had attempted suicide only to fail, merely breaking his leg in the process. Assigned to his case, she knew it best to make contact as soon as possible, before he had a chance to think about what he had done and come up with some story to cover the reason behind his actions.

As Angela passed her key-card through the slot and entered the long hallway into the Psych Unit, Karman approached her. "Doctor, I hear you're taking on the Hannigan patient. I want to be part of your team on this one, if that would be all right with you."

Angela paused, gave Karman a quick once-over. It then hit her: this was the woman she had envisioned and been told about. As she nodded, their eyes locked in recognition, each remembering their own vision of the other, their own prophecy of what was to come.

"I'd welcome the opportunity to work with you, Miss, uh?"

"It's Karman, Karman Sheldon."

"Yes, I've heard of your work with the patients. You're a bit of a legend, known for your ability to produce results; not an easy task in this ward, I'm afraid. May I have the patient's chart? I want to look it over and then we'll pay him a visit."

As Angela followed, Karman walked to the reception area, produced Euclid's chart and handed it to her. "I'll call you when I'm ready, Karman, "stated Angela and she headed off to the privacy of her office.

It wasn't much of an office. Just an old wooden desk and chair, the room sparsely adorned with a few watercolor paintings donated by the local artists. A lamp stood on the right side of the desk and a plastic in/out box on the left.

Angela read the chart. Euclid Hannigan, age fifty-nine, widower, unemployed, no prior mental problems, possible suicide attempt, no history of violence, taking no medication prior to the event. This would certainly be interesting, if nothing else. What would drive an otherwise stable man to attempt to end his life? Money? Loss of his wife?

Depression? Chemical imbalance?

She hit the call button and summoned Karman to the office. "Karman, I initially ask the patient various questions to get a take on his present state of mind and how far I may safely go with my inquiries. I'm assuming you've already met this patient since you requested to be part of the team. What was your observation?"

"Funny thing about this man, he's in great spirits, very cordial, and seems to be in control of his senses; no outbursts or outward signs of depression. The only thing he complained about was the pain associated with his leg fracture. We gave him a morphine shot about two hours ago. I haven't heard a peep from him since."

"Let's go see him. He should be ready for another shot to ease the pain."

As she'd suspected, Euclid was alert and showing some discomfort when they entered his room. Angela neared his bed and was astonished to recognize the man's face. Why, of course, she thought, these are the two people I was told I'd meet, Euclid and Karman. It made complete sense. She couldn't hide her excitement at finally being face to face with the friends she'd envisioned. Angela drew closer to her patient's bedside.

"Hello, Mr. Hannigan, I'm Dr. Frank. How are you feeling this afternoon?"

Euclid turned his face toward the doctor's and froze. Before him stood a young wisp of a woman with long blonde hair and green eyes. This was the other woman he had seen in his dream, the young pretty one. Still staring into her face, he managed to stutter, "H-h-hi, Doc. I'm fe-fe-feeling okay 'cept for my leg hurtin' something fierce. Sure got myself into a mess this time, didn't I?"

"We'll give you something to ease your physical pain. That's the easy part." Angela turned toward Karman, motioning her to hand the patient a Vicodin tablet. As Euclid accepted the pill, she poured a glass of water and handed it to him. His hand shook a bit as he brought the glass to his lips, a bit of water splashing down his face and onto the hospital gown.

"That should take care of your discomfort." Angela took one of Euclid's large hands in hers, patted it and candidly asked, "Are you up to answering some questions?"

Euclid looked away in shame as the memory of the morning surfaced.

"Doc, I ain't crazy. Dunno why I did such a plumb stupid thing. Just I've been havin' strange things happen lately. If I tell 'em to ya, you'll surely think me mad. I'm afraid to tell ya. I swear on my late wife Gracie's grave, I'm not some nut."

"No need to be afraid of me, Mr. Hannigan. I'm here to help you get well both in mind and body. Something drove you to a state where you felt your only way out was to take your life. From what I've been told, you attempted to hang yourself but the rope broke. Lucky for you, I would say. Why did you feel this was the answer to your problem?"

Euclid heaved a large sigh, glanced at Karman who urged him on with a nod of her head, summoned every ounce of courage he had in him and proceeded to tell Angela about the voices and visions. Amazingly, she looked relieved and not at all shocked by his confessions. Dare he tell her more? Would she be as understanding of a man who taunted others with e-mails, phone calls and DVD's? Had he the fortitude to come clean with it all? What would she think of old Euclid then?

DEJA VU

What a familiar story Mr. Euclid Hannigan told; not unlike the visions and voices she had been experiencing lately. He certainly had his share of heartache with the loss of his wife, and being laid off from a lifelong job didn't help the situation. She sensed he was holding back, not telling her the entire story. Euclid would go so far and then clam up. She saw it in his face and in his eyes, the fear of revealing the truth.

A voice interrupted her thoughts, saying, "Angela, it's time. This is the moment to unite. Be not afraid to speak honestly and openly to Karman."

This message was a welcome relief. In fact, it was exactly what she had wanted to do since she laid eyes on Karman. But how would she approach her? *Just do it*, rang in her mind. Yeah, thought Angela, easy to say, but she could be jeopardizing her entire career.

Trust your instincts. They are the only thing that is real.

"Okay, okay, I got it," Angela said aloud. She bent over her desk, pressed the intercom button on the phone, saying, "Karman, please come to my office," and sat back in her chair, apprehensive but feeling more alive than she had felt in years.

Karman gently rapped on the office door before entering. "You wanted to see me?"

"Yes, Karman, please take a seat," Angela said, directing Karman to the chair facing her.

Seeking a 'read' on Karman, Angela searched her face. Recognition passed between the two women once again. If only Karman would be the one to make the first move so she knew the feelings she had were reciprocated. This was going to be difficult. How could she simply blurt out that she'd seen the woman in visions and had messages to reveal to her? Again the voice, *Just do it*.

Angela leaned back in her chair, exhaled, looked deep into Karman's eyes and in a soft, gentle voice said, "Before you react to what I'm going to tell you, please hear me out. You must promise to keep what I'm going to reveal to you in strict confidence."

"That goes without saying," Karman replied.

"Several times I have dreamt of meeting you, Karman, along with our patient, Euclid Hannigan. I've been told we're destined to fulfill a mission that is greater than any of us; an undertaking that will change many lives."

Karman's face changed from wonder to understanding. She scooted her chair closer to the front of the desk, leaned forward and whispered, "Doc, I hate to interrupt you but everything you say to me now is what I've been hesitant to speak of. I recognized Euclid as soon as I saw his face, and then when you arrived, well, let's just say I was floored. You see, Dr. Frank, I had visions of the two of you also. Messages came to me saying we would meet and I would understand once we spoke. I was fearful you would get a key and lock me up in a padded cell should I approach you with this information. Thank you so much for breaking the ice. I couldn't figure out a way to bring the subject up to you."

A broad smile spread across each woman's face as they acknowledged a kinship and camaraderie which ran deep into their souls. Words were unnecessary. Each knew her purpose and reason.

"Karman, it appears we have yet one other person to confront. I noticed the attraction between you and Mr. Hannigan. Those side glances and deep looks exchanged. How do you feel about speaking with him of the dreams and visions?"

"Not a problem, Doc. I get the sense Euclid is not being completely honest with us. He's talked with me of the visions and dreams as he has you. When I've pressed further, asking if they brought him to the brink of suicide, he simply doesn't answer. It's as though he doesn't want to recognize the reason. Normally, I would never, ever try to counsel a patient, but some force compelled me forward; I knew it was what I was meant to do."

"Believe me, Karman, I understand completely. There is an explanation for the bond you and Euclid have formed, have no doubt about it. You have my express permission to delve deeper into his psyche; just remember to report back your findings. I realize once he finds a trusting friend in you, he will be ready to speak openly with me."

Karman nodded in accord with the doctor's wishes, rose from her chair and headed toward the door. An unbreakable bond had been created, forever linking the two women's lives.

"By the way, Karman, I think you can call me Angela now."

"Will do, Doc – I mean Angela." Karman giggled a bit as the new friendship began to take form.

THE GOOD FRIEND

"What in Sam Hill have you gone and done, my friend," asked Harry as he approached Euclid's bedside. "You had me greatly concerned, especially since I went and sold you that rifle."

"Ah, Harry, just plain foolishness on my part, that's all t'was. Don't worry your mind 'bout it. Wasn't your fault. Ya were just being a good pal. Yer friend Euclid has learned his lesson. Ain't never gonna do something so stupid again."

"That better be a promise, and I want that rifle back as soon as you get out of this place. I'll refund you the full amount you paid me, but I won't rest until its back in my shop."

"Sure, Harry. I don't have no need for a rifle. Should have my head examined for ever doin' such a foolish thing. Oh, that's right, I am havin' my head examined." Euclid let out a roar of laughter, once more sounding of his old self.

Harry joined in on the joke and knew, in that instant, he had no need to worry about his friend, though he did make a mental note to visit and check in on him often. Loneliness could devastate a person.

Euclid and Harry spent another twenty minutes chatting. Harry encouraging Euclid to think about working in his store part-time, and Euclid was thrilled to realize what a wonderful friend he had in Harry. After Harry left, promising to call him soon, he couldn't help but think everything **had** happened for a reason, just like the voices told him. Nope, no mistake about it. He wanted more than anything to talk with Karman but feared her reaction. After all, she was a nurse in a crazy house. Before this line of thinking went further, he realized he was not alone. There, sitting at the foot of his hospital bed, sat Gina. Ah, how beautiful she looked. This time he was not at all afraid and welcomed her visit.

"Euclid, dear sweet Euclid, what on earth have you done? Your poor leg, does it bring you much discomfort?"

"Just a bit Gina. I was wantin' to be with you again. Foolish thinkin' from a silly old man, wasn't it?" How much he wished to feel her body against his and seek comfort in her embrace.

It was like she read his mind. In her sweet, angelic voice, she told him this was her last visit with him. It was time for him to move on in his life, to find another companion, to fulfill his purpose. He balked at her words; he wanted only Gina, no one else. She had been his life for such a long time. He could not fathom anyone else filling her shoes. *"Sweetheart, the time has come for me to leave you. There is no more I can achieve with my visits. I've told you what is to come. Be the brave, courageous, kind man I married. Of you I am proud. I realize the difficulty you face. This has been hard to accept and I now see you do understand the importance of your destiny. You met the women who will join this mission, so my job here is complete. It is now up to you to follow through. I love you, Euclid, and because of this love, I ask you to go on with your life. Allow the love and friendships offered. That is what will please me. Your happiness is my concern. As long as you hold on to what you had without seeing what you can have, I will not be able to rest in peace. Help me, love, to find the harmony I seek. Promise me this and I'll watch over you with pleasure and contentment."*

With tears streaming down his face, Euclid replied, "Gina, I will do what ya ask of me if it will bring ya the peace ya desire. Before ya leave me, I needs to ask ya, was it you who saved me from myself? Did ya cut the rope and empty the rifle of bullets?"

Gina's magical laughter filled the air as she said, "Oh, Euclid, it was not I who saved you, but yourself who did so. I have no power to change what is inside your soul. You will understand these things once this journey has ended. I must go now. I bid you well."

Euclid flinched, his heart full of pain, as he saw his beloved wife was no longer at his side. A voice startled him as his nurse Karman entered the room.

"How are you feeling, Mr. Hannigan? Need some more pain medication?"

Yes, indeed, he thought. It was exactly what he needed. Yup, exactly what the doctor ordered.

CONFESSIONS BETWEEN FRIENDS

Karman sat at the nurses' station and glanced at the clock on the wall. She was eager to confront Euclid about the reason behind his actions but didn't want to speak with him until he was fully awake, alert, and in control of his senses. His medication would be wearing off within the next ten to fifteen minutes. She made a mental note to drop in on him in a half hour. For now, she had rounds to make and other patients to tend to.

A searing pain stabbed through Euclid's leg, instantly waking him from his slumber. He grimaced, leaned upright, and reached for his leg, as if that would take away the discomfort. "Ah," Euclid thought, 'Ya deserve this punishment, ya old fool." He wondered if he should ask for more medication or just 'take it like a man'. He didn't like the feeling of being medicated; it dulled his wits. On the other hand, he knew he could only take so much pain before giving into it. Maybe if he called that nurse, Karman, she'd take his mind off his physical problems. Just as he reached for the buzzer, in Karman walked, right on cue.

"No need for pressing that buzzer, I'm here. I knew you'd be waking up soon, Euclid," stated Karman as she entered his room. "Are you feeling much discomfort?"

"Not so much now you're here," Euclid answered with a twinkle in his eye.

"Flattery will get you everywhere," Karman responded, pleased her patient seemed in good spirits.

She walked toward Euclid, pulling the chair as close to the bed as possible. She leaned toward him, peered straight into his face, and stated, "Mr. Hannigan, we already know you attempted suicide, not once, but twice, correct?"

Euclid's face flushed bright red, embarrassed by his actions. He nodded in agreement.

"You listen, now, and hear me out before saying anything."

Her patient's body rose a bit off the bed and his face showed strain as a surge of pain coursed through his leg.

"I'd prefer you be awake and aware to hear what I am about to say.

Can you stay with me that long, Euclid, before you need pain medication?"

Her patient mouthed the word yes as sweat formed on his temples.

"Euclid, you have to believe me when I tell you that you are not some crazy guy because of the visions and messages. On the contrary, it's completely sane and rational. Dr.Frank and I have also been experiencing visions and messages. In fact, we recognized each other as soon as we met, as well as remembering you. Didn't you feel an instant connection between us?"

Liberation showed on Euclid's face, the freedom to finally speak the truth without fear of reprisal. "Karman, I knew ya as soon as I saw your face and heard ya speak. The voice told me I was gonna meet ya and that doctor lady, too. It kept tellin' me it was my destiny and I'd know who ya were when we met."

Karman took Euclid's hand in hers, pressed it softly, leaned over and placed a supple kiss on his forehead. He smiled, accepting this touch of affection so long needed.

"Now, my friend, I feel you are holding something back, afraid to share something with us. Is this true or a figment of my imagination?"

Beads of perspiration fell down Euclid's face. He knew it was now or never. What would this newfound friend think of him once he revealed his ghastly deeds? Would she be so welcoming once the truth was told? *Tell her, Euclid. It is safe. She will understand; it is what you must do.*

After inhaling the biggest breathe of his life, Euclid moved nearer Karman and confessed all: the phone calls to Joshua, the DVD sent to Rosie, and the e-mails to Monty. Instead of horror, Karman reacted with understanding, compassion, and interest.

"I know that was very difficult for you, Euclid. And I do have one more thing to ask of you. Will you repeat this to Dr. Frank? If we three are to accomplish our mission, we must be forthright and truthful, holding nothing back."

Euclid nodded his head once more in agreement. Fact was, he felt his heart open up with joy now that his purpose mirrored that of his new friends. It was all falling into place.

Karman handed a pain pill to Euclid, which he accepted with gratitude, before saying, "Now get some sleep so you can gain strength.

We have much to accomplish in a very short amount of time. This I know for a fact." With a wave of her hand, Karman exited the room, eager to contact Angela with the good news.

Angela received Karman's report with enthusiasm, yet realized time was short. First thing she needed to do was check in on Euclid to see how he was progressing and to hear his tale for herself. It was five p.m. What she had not communicated to either Euclid or Karman was the urgency of action. If Euclid capable, she would be asking him and Karman to meet with her the next morning.

To Angela's delight, Euclid felt able to be released, just so he had a bit of medication to ease his discomfort. She and Euclid talked for hours, during which time a bond of alliance to their mutual endeavor had formed. After Angela signed his discharge papers for the next morning, Euclid agreed, to meet at Angela's office, accompanied by Karman, eleven a.m. sharp.

Exhilaration.

AN EVENING WITH THE FRANKS

Angela arrived home from the hospital to find her girls arguing over a cookie.

"Alicia, Alexis, stop arguing this minute," she snapped, tired from the day's work. "We have one cookie left. Either you two break it in half and share it or neither of you will get any, do you understand me?" Getting no response, Angela repeated, "I said, do you understand me?"

"Yes Mommy, we understand," replied Alexis as she broke the cookie in two.

"Hey, your half is bigger than mine," said Alicia as her sister handed her the piece of cookie.

"It is not," Alexis retorted.

"Is so," was her sister's immediate reply.

Angela snatched both pieces of cookie from her daughters' hands, crushed them on the table, saying, "That does it. Nobody gets a cookie".

The girls began to cry.

"No crying, either, or you're both going up to your room. You have to learn to share and be happy with what you get. Now I don't want to hear one more peep out of your mouths. Go on in to the family room and join your dad."

"Yes, Mommy," they gloomily replied through pouting lips, rising from their seats and leaving the kitchen.

Angela felt a bit guilty after being so harsh with the girls. It broke her heart to see their sad little faces and tears in their eyes. Being a responsible parent was not an easy task, but she was not going to raise spoiled brats, dammit!

What a day! First the strange phone call for Monty, then meeting Euclid Hannigan and Karman. The whole day had been bizarre. Monty had finally expressed his true thoughts and feelings about showing kindness to a fellow man. This sudden truthfulness seemed to alter the love she felt for him; it was not as deep or as pure. She felt used and deceived. It was though he said and did the things he knew she wanted him to say and do, not what he really felt or believed. In fact, she was now married to a stranger. He was so loving and caring within his own family. No one could ask for a better husband and father. Yes, he did work hard and provide for the family, but at what cost to others? That was the problem.

As Angela wrestled with these emotions, she heard a voice saying, "Do not believe all you see, especially with Monty. Love for family is nice, but he will have to pay the price if he turns his back on humanity. Time will tell. Remember, I am by your side always. I am fair to those who listen. I am here for those who seek."

Music played in the background; the same music she'd been hearing for weeks.

She didn't fight the voice this time; she was beginning to understand. She simply was required to be alert, patient, and, most of all, listen.

Angela joined the others, now watching TV in the family room. As she entered the room, Monty glanced at his wife, hoping to sense her mood. He feared losing her. That was why he'd never explained his true feelings about helping others. What he felt, in his heart and soul, was that each person was responsible for their own life. He never asked for handouts, so why should he give them to strangers, or, for that matter, even friends? To a large degree, he was pompous and felt superior to those who hadn't reached the success in life he had attained. Why shouldn't he feel this way? After all, he was the one who built his business. Nobody helped him. No one cared if he had food on the table or a roof over his head. What he had in life, he earned.

He had always known Angela held a completely opposite point of view. She lived her life with such purpose. She would give money to beggars, donate canned goods to the hungry, and volunteer at the local food bank, doing anything she could to help the needy. Now she was intent on providing free psychiatric counseling to those nut cases. Secretly, he felt her foolish and naïve to believe her actions would do much good. These people were users and losers, nothing else. He loved her so much that he'd never dared to tell her his own point of view. Now, however, it was out in the open.

That damned Bracken! I should have called him back, Monty thought to himself, blaming Bracken for his own lack of action. The main problem, as he saw it, was that he'd always agreed with her on this matter of aiding others, which couldn't have been further from the way he felt. He knew she wanted someone with deep compassion, so he became that person. Well, at least in front of her. In his business life, he was heartless.

Monty noticed Angela chose to sit in the recliner and not next to him. He just couldn't read her. She didn't seem angry or upset. In fact, she had a peaceful air about her and there was a touch of a smile on her face. She looked as if she was in her own world, lost in deep thought. Well, thought Monty, better to leave her alone. She'll talk about this when she's ready. I'm certainly not going to push the subject. Hell, no.

There was high tension in the air. In truth, the only family members really watching TV were the twins. Monty couldn't help but glance Angela's way every few minutes. He wasn't able to concentrate on the show; couldn't even tell what it was the girls were watching.

For a split second, Angela clicked eyes with him. In that instant Monty knew he was in for the fight of his life.

The fight for his family.

NO OPEN HOUSE FOR YOU, MY DEAR

Rosie stood naked in front of the full-length mirror in her bedroom. She found herself unable to speak or do anything but let out one loud, piercing scream.

She peered closer at her underarms and inner thighs, turning her body a bit, seeing the same greenish-brown scaly skin down her spine and the back of her knees. Her hand trembled when she placed it at the nape of her neck. She felt repulsed as she touched the scales, feeling their coarseness.

A sob caught in her throat. Her face reflected astonishment, bewilderment, and shock. This was too much for her to handle alone. She was turning into some kind of freak! "What is happening to me?" The reality of her situation hit, hard, and she stated flatly, "This whole thing is a nightmare." A multitude of thoughts entered her mind. *Should I call a doctor? Should I call my dear friend Rita? What about the Open House scheduled tomorrow?*

Rosie Richards, a woman strong and sure of herself, was barely able to pick up her cell phone and call the After Hours Clinic. Her hand unsteady, her body quivered as she entered the phone number, one digit at a time.

After a few rings, the clinic's secretary answered, "Raleigh After Hours Clinic, how may I assist you? "

"Miss, I need to get in today to see someone. I don't know what is going on. My skin is changing and it seems to be spreading," explained Rosie. "

"Have you been here before?"

"No, Miss, I haven't."

After giving the secretary her name and phone number, she was instructed to stop by within the hour and the doctor would see her.

The next person Rosie called was Fred Baxter. Her call went to his voice-mail, so she left a message asking him to cover the Open House tomorrow and to call her back as soon as possible. With that done, Rosie threw on a pair of slacks, a long-sleeved turtleneck top, left her hair down, and hurried out the door without even bothering to put on her usual gobs of makeup.

Within five minutes, she arrived at the clinic. Hope there isn't a long wait, she thought.

She was fortunate; there were only two people in the waiting room when she arrived, a woman who was coughing her head off and a teenager who was supporting his left arm with his right hand. She walked up to the reception station and said, "I'm Rosie Richards. I called a few minutes ago."

"Oh, yes, Ms. Richards. I remember," the young woman at the reception desk replied.

She walked to a file cabinet, took out some papers and handed them to Rosie saying,

"I need these filled out and a copy of your insurance card. The doctor will see you shortly."

"Thank you," Rosie responded as she took the pile of papers and headed to the nearest chair to fill them out. She watched as a woman wearing medical scrubs entered the waiting area and motioned the coughing woman to follow her. "Shouldn't be long now, I suppose," Rosie said to the young man, who appeared to be in quite a bit of pain, judging from the grimace on his face.

He nodded, saying, "I sure hope not".

She went back to filling out the paperwork. Geez, she thought to herself, all this stuff to fill out just to see a doctor; sure was different years ago. She completed the paperwork, handed it to the receptionist and went back to her seat.

Approximately twenty minutes later, the nurse appeared again and called the young man to see the doctor.

The Women's Wonder Day book she had open before her was a mere blur. She'd read and then re-read the same sentence, unable to comprehend the meaning of the words. Looking at this book did nothing to calm her nerves. The only thing that could ease the anxiety was an answer, a logical medical reason for the skin condition. Not conscious of her actions, Rosie glanced at the door leading into the patient area every few minutes, hopeful the nurse would appear and call her name. She needed to talk to someone who would provide a quick fix to the malformations on her skin.

After fifteen minutes or so, the young man she had spoken with in the waiting room came through the door. Rosie knew she was next. A wave of hope filled her body when the nurse appeared and beckoned Rosie to follow her.

"Hello, Ms. Richards," she said in a professional tone. She told Rosie she needed her weight and to take her blood pressure. Today, even getting her weight read didn't bother Rosie. All she wanted was this part over with and to see the doctor.

Following the nurse, whose name badge said Terri, over to the scale, Rosie lifted herself onto the base and watched as Terri slid the upper scale weight to the 200 pound slot. The scale arm moved completely down on the right side until the nurse slid the upper weight to the 250 pound slot and adjusted the lower scale weight to 28 pounds. With that done, it was now in perfect balance. Rosie stepped down from the scales base and watched as the nurse wrote down her weight: two hundred seventy-eight pounds.

"We're going to put you in this room." Terri motioned to Rosie as she opened the second door to her right. "I see by your chart that you have a rash of some sort that's bothering you; is that correct," inquired the nurse as she read a piece of paper clipped to a metal board held in her hand.

"Yes, Miss. It started today and I can't for the life of me figure out why".

"I'm sure the doctor will answer any questions you have. He should be along shortly. Now remove your clothes and slip this gown over your shoulders," she instructed and handed Rosie a flimsy paper gown. "I'll be back in a moment to take your blood pressure before the doctor arrives."

Rosie nodded she understood. A short while later, the nurse returned and slipped the blood pressure sleeve up Rosie's left arm and began pumping air through it. She frowned upon seeing a reading of 165 over 101 and asked Rosie if she ever had such high blood pressure before.

"No, Miss. It may have been a bit borderline. Why, what is it reading now?"

Terri told Rosie the figures and suggested the doctor might be able to help in that area also. Not wanting to continue the conversation, Rosie simply answered, "Yeah, good," while thinking that with what she'd been experiencing lately, it was a wonder her blood pressure wasn't even higher. The nurse left the room as Rosie climbed onto the examination bed, which had that same flimsy paper wrapped around its middle. She sat nervously swinging her legs back and forth, wondering how long it would be before the doc showed up.

Within ten minutes, a young-looking dark-skinned man with black hair and steel-framed glasses entered the examination room. He peered over his glasses, glimpsed the forlorn woman sitting on his examining table, picked up her chart and stated, "Good afternoon, Ms. Richards. My name is Dr, Sabistarian. What seems to be the problem?"

"Doc," Rosie responded while exposing her arm, "this stuff just appeared on my body. It's on my legs, neck, back, and inside thighs, too."

Dr. Sabistarian took Rosie's arm, trying in vain to conceal his surprise at her affliction. The physician ran his gloved fingers over the surface of the scaly skin and asked,

" How long have you had these eruptions?" Without waiting for a reply, he continued, "Does it give you any discomfort?"

Fact was, he had never seen such a condition, nor had he been taught about this particular form of dermatitis while attending medical school or during his internship, residency, or any other training that he could recall. It repulsed and interested him at the same time. The scales resembled those of a reptile yet were in apparent harmony with the uninfected areas of her skin. There was no transition area; rather, the scales seemed to be a perfectly normal part of her body. Further tests were a must, he decided.

It seemed that this was now her 'normal' skin; nothing but blood vessels and muscle underneath it, as if she'd undergone a metamorphism of sorts, which was, of course, impossible to imagine. It intrigued him and, with reluctant fascination, he proceeded to examine the other parts of her body the scales now covered.

"It doesn't hurt at all. I noticed it today, this morning when having my coffee. Well, Doc, what is it? Can you give me something to make it disappear? I have to look presentable. I'm a realtor. I can't go running around town meeting clients with this ugly stuff on my body. Doc, you must do something to help me here," Rosie pleaded, hoping to get an immediate cure.

"So it doesn't itch or burn and it appeared this morning. Are you allergic to any foods, cleaning products such as soap, detergent or cosmetics," Dr. Sabistarian asked.

"I have never been allergic to anything in my life, Doc. It wasn't there yesterday and all I had to eat yesterday was a hamburger, fries, and some doughnuts. Nothing I haven't eaten before."

In an effort to put his patient at ease, Dr. Sabistarian told Rosie, "Ms Richards, before I am able to make the proper diagnosis, I will require some tests to be done, including a complete blood workup. For now, I'm going to prescribe an ointment to be applied three times a day over the areas. Are you allergic to medications that you know of?"

"No, Doctor, nothing," said Rosie.

After filing out a prescription form, the doctor handed it to Rosie along with the name and number of the local medical center. "I'll have my receptionist make an appointment so we can get a few tests run. She'll set you up an appointment with me for the following week."

Rosie looked at the young physician's face and, as their eyes met, the doctor averted his glance, hoping this patient hadn't seen the apprehension and concern he was sure it showed.

Not knowing what else to say, Dr. Sabistarian told Rosie he would see her again, and to be sure and apply the ointment he had prescribed. This was so unique, he didn't know if he would ever find a good explanation. Recognizing he must give this poor woman some hope, he attempted a bit of comfort by saying, "We'll await the test results, Ms. Richards. They should tell us something, okay?"

Discouraged, Rosie simply nodded her head. She certainly had not received the answers she needed. Her courage, once so strong, was replaced with fearfulness; her strength traded for weakness.

LESSONS SOON BE LEARNED

He lay on the kitchen floor, feeling so alone. For the first time in his life he needed a helping hand, a comforting voice, an act of kindness. Who could he turn to? There really wasn't anyone. He'd broken off relationships with his family years ago and turned his back on the lot of them. They were a bunch of scavengers, coming to him in need of money for an operation or because little Carl required new shoes or they were going to lose their home. Blah, blah, blah, such sad tales of woe. It made him sick how they kissed his butt believing it would change his mind. Who did they think he was, Santa Claus? He wasn't responsible for their happiness. All in the name of love for family. If that was love, he wanted no part of it. As far as Joshua was concerned, he had no family; just a bunch of vultures. He owed them nothing and he asked nothing of them in return. Beth was the only family member he had truly loved, and look what became of her. Joshua pushed himself into a sitting position against the kitchen cabinet. As he gazed at the floor around him, his eyes opened wide. Sitting in individual piles were what remained of his hair, once a rich, thick mane in which he took such pride. Instinctively, Joshua grasped his head, yearning for the sensation of the plush locks against his hands. He felt, instead, a smooth bald scalp. Jerking his hands away, he shuffled to his feet and ran toward the nearest mirror. For a few seconds, he was unable to move, paralyzed and shocked by the reflection. Filled with panic and urgency, he began pacing back and forth, muttering, "It can't be. This isn't happening to me."

Joshua leaned against the hallway wall gazing into nothingness, unable to focus or comprehend. As daylight turned into dusk, he remained propped against the wall, blankly staring at naught in the now dark vestibule. His vacant mind sought protection from the unimaginable, the unbelievable, the inconceivable.

Slowly, thoughts surfaced as remembrance of the horrific events that brought Joshua Allen to his senses once again. He turned on the dining room light and rushed to the nearest mirror. "No! Oh, my God, no," came a delirious scream. He clutched at various parts of his body to prove to himself they were genuine. In place of his thick black mane of hair he found long tufts of coarse red fur. The new hair protruded from his chin and cheeks and encircled his lips. He spat out bits of long strands that invaded his gaping mouth. Red, hair-like growth sprouted from various places on his once-bald head, around his ears, and down the nape of his neck. He grabbed at the hairy fur, pulled on it as if it were some grotesque Halloween mask now glued to his skin.

Joshua cast his eyes downward and became aware of this same growth shooting out of his wrists and arms. "My God," he cried as he ripped off his cashmere sweater and cast it to the floor, exposing the muscled chest now blanketed with the same growth of long furry hair. A groan came from deep within followed by hysterical, mad laughter as his mind failed to find sanity or purpose.

"Steady Joshua, get a hold of your wits, must call Joansie," he mumbled trying to rationalize under such surreal conditions. Yeah, Joansie would help him out. She said to call her no matter what. She'd believe him now that he was some sort of freak, some monstrous werewolf like creature. *Proof's in the pudding, my dear, isn't it?* Joshua chuckled to himself. Sanity now completely gone, he walked to the kitchen, fumbling as he turned on the light and located his cell phone, earlier tossed with his keys and wallet on the counter. With intent, Joshua picked up his cell, which instantaneously sent him reeling backward across the room with an electrifying force.

In his haste to call Joansie for help, the memory of his last contact with the cell phone had slipped his mind. "No! No! No! Ahhhhhhhhh," he screeched as electric shocks surged through his body. He held his head in his hands, sobbing tears of terror and frustration. Joshua remained on the floor, gulping for air, the Valium still in his pocket.

SCENTS OR NONSENSE

Sleep did not come easily for Monty or Angela Frank. Unspoken words and unshared thoughts created an atmosphere of tension so thick it filled the room.

Angela lay in their bed next to her husband and hoped he would not reach for her this night. Not that she felt repulsion for him; rather, she had mixed emotions about their entire relationship. There were the voices that warned her to keep silent and not share the visions or dreams with Monty. She was beginning to understand the reason why. The man she had loved and cared for hid behind a mask of deceit and lies. His true self had emerged, and what he had revealed this afternoon she did not like at all. Had she shared the dreams, the visions, or the meeting scheduled for morning with Euclid and Karman, she knew he would have laughed it off, criticized her for allowing herself to buy into such things.

Angela yearned with all her heart to be able to talk with Monty, to hold his hand and open up about all of it. She knew what was happening with her was huge and had purpose, importance, and meaning. Oh, my Monty, she thought, I see you give great love to your family. I know the good in you. If only you could understand, we are more than our family. We are brother and sister to every single person on earth. She would not give up on him yet.

At that moment, Angela knew she was meant to teach him the real meaning of love. It would be up to him to choose which path to follow.

Monty Frank knew he should be taking his wife in his arms, promising to turn a new leaf and swearing to try to be a better neighbor and citizen. What she did not seem to realize was he would have to give up his livelihood, his income, his business, in order to do that. He knew nothing else and had worked for years to build the success he held today. The cold, hard fact was he loved his business. It was easy; there were hundreds of new prospects at his fingertips each day. He could work from home and be there for the kids and her when they needed him. She expected him to feel guilty or ashamed of taking advantage of the weak, the downtrodden, and the helpless. He just didn't feel the same way. In all honesty, dealing with these pathetic people gave him a rush of adrenalin he couldn't imagine getting anywhere else. He felt powerful, commanding, and superior as he took over their finances.

It was a game to see how many he could reel in to sign a contract with him. In fact, what he loved most was calling, e-mailing, and harassing those who contacted him for help. He wouldn't let up, going after them, wearing them down, and reasoning with them until they were convinced his plan was the only way to get out of their dire straits.

He never let Angela know about this part of his business. She believed the people sought him out and cheerfully set up a debt payment plan. Most did so hesitantly and after much persuasion. Still, he felt nothing but pleasure from his work. Now he feared he was going to have to choose between his family and this business; he could not imagine giving up either.

"Geez, Louise, what is that horrid smell?" Angela asked as she vaulted upright, breaking the dead silence between husband and wife. "Monty, oh, my gosh, it smells like something died and rotted, Ugh gross! Monty, did you let off gas again because if you did and it smells this bad, you are going to the doctor."

"No, Ang, it wasn't me. Matter of fact, I've been smelling something weird, too. Thought it was a skunk or something coming through the open window."

Angela jumped up from the bed, holding her nose closed with her fingers, and went over to the window and shut it tight. Instead of the odor going away, it grew stronger. As she approached the bed, the stench became overwhelming. She bravely sniffed the covers and linens, which gave off a lavender scent. As she grew closer to Monty, the full force of the smell hit her smack in the face. She gagged and coughed saying, "Monty, it's you! Oh, my gosh, I can't sleep here. Go take a shower. Do something; it's making me ill."

"Jesus Christ, Angela, if I take a shower I'll be wide awake. It ain't me," Monty growled.

"Monty James Frank, it is too you. How can you not smell that awful odor on your body? I don't care what you say, you are taking a shower or I'm sleeping on the couch tonight and I mean it!" Angela angrily responded.

Monty got out of bed, turned to Angela and barked, "Okay, okay, I'll take a shower if it will make you happy. I'm telling you it ain't me, though." He grabbed a towel from the linen closet and headed toward the adjoining bathroom. Angela opened the window a crack, now confident she had found the source of the repulsive smell.

Monty turned on the shower and adjusted the temperature until the water streamed a pleasing lukewarm to the touch. He'd never been fond of hot showers, preferring the water on the cool side. As he lathered up the washcloth, he couldn't help but notice the smell did seem to follow him. It was much stronger when he sniffed his arms than when he sniffed away from his body. Ugh! What a repulsive odor it was, just like a skunk would smell. He wondered how on earth this was possible. After the walk he took with the girls, he hadn't noticed any odor. It wasn't until later this evening. Just didn't make any sense at all. But, then, many things weren't making sense these days.

As he scrubbed his body, Monty realized he still smelled that horrid stench. Perhaps he should be using something stronger than the antibacterial soap to wash with. He'd read somewhere that hydrogen peroxide, baking soda and dish soap worked on skunk spray, while the tomato juice remedy only covered it up. Christ, he thought, this is all I need. What a lousy day. Monty continued to scrub, rub, and wash his entire body including his hair and scalp. After coming out of the shower, he proceeded to dry off his body and hoped with all his heart that the smell was gone. No such luck. Though a bit less intense, the skunk smell was definitely on his body.

As he entered the bedroom, he told Angela, "I'll need some peroxide, baking soda, and dish soap. That shower didn't take it away. Will you get it for me, hon?"

Angela looked at her naked husband standing in front of her, the pitiful and pleading look on his face, and had to giggle. She wondered how in the world he had managed to find a skunk. And leave it to him to get sprayed. "Honey, I'll be right back with them. Do you know how much we're supposed to use?"

"Not really," Monty replied, "but I figure heavy on the peroxide and baking soda and a little of the dish soap will do."

Angela went to the medicine cabinet in the hallway, took out the bottle of peroxide and walked downstairs to the kitchen. She turned on the light, found the baking soda in the cupboard and the dish soap underneath the kitchen sink. Using Monty's suggestion, she mixed almost a quart of the peroxide with a quarter cup of the baking soda and a healthy squirt of the dish soap. *Hope this works,* she thought. The idea of lying next to her husband if he stilled reeked sent shivers down her spine. She just wouldn't be able to stand it. Angela mixed the ingredients to her satisfaction and headed up the stairs.

"All right, Monty. Here it is," she said as she entered the bedroom. "I'll help you put it on your back and the areas you can't reach but you're going to have to do the rest."

Monty readily agreed and allowed Angela to wash his back with the mixture. After she had finished, she handed the bottle to Monty. He went back into the bathroom, set on getting this ordeal over and done. Monty scrubbed, washed, and rubbed the remainder of his body and head with the mixture, anxious to feel and smell clean once again. At last, he had completed the monumental chore and sniffed his arms to confirm the remedy had worked its magic. Not only had it not worked, the smell was worse than ever. So horrid, in fact, he felt waves of nausea hit him. His face turned ghostly white. Unable to control himself, Monty heaved his stomach contents into the toilet bowl. He heard Angela calling to him, "Monty, what's going on? Are you okay?" He didn't have the strength to yell back and as Angela came into the bathroom, he answered in a weak, feeble voice, "Ang, it didn't work. It smells worse. I gotta get rid of this stuff. I'm sick as a dog."

Angela consoled Monty and led him to their bed while fighting the urge to be sick to her own stomach. He is so right, she thought, the smell has become much stronger. The first thing on their agenda tomorrow morning would be a trip to the After Hours Clinic. It opened at 8:00 a.m. and they'd be on the doorstep.

Angela turned to Monty, saw the color was starting to return to his face and said, "Sweetie, I love you but I cannot stay in this room with you tonight. I just can't handle the stench. Hope you understand."

He nodded his head. He understood. How could he expect anybody to be in the same room with him? He couldn't even stand to be in the same room with himself.

Angela blew Monty a kiss, promised to get him to the doctor in the morning, closed their bedroom door and went to the linen closet to gather a blanket, pillow, and sheets before heading downstairs to the couch.

What a relief to breath in the sweet smell of citrus and lavender from the diffusers she had placed in the bookshelf and cabinet in the family room. She had never cherished a scent a much as she did at that moment.

After she folded the sheets under the cushions, Angela plumped her pillow, lay down on the comfy couch, stretched out her legs, pulled the blanket over her body and adjusted her position until she felt at ease. A familiar voice rang in her ear. This time she was alert and ready to hear the message. Angela laid her head in the middle of the down-filled pillow and closed her eyes.

A melodic symphony, that magical music played in her head. A soft, tender, soothing, clear voice came through saying, "You have learned much of your husband's soul today. His road will be the one he chooses to travel; you cannot prevent what will come to be. It shall be the destiny he selects. Turn to your children, your work, your passion, and much good will come forth. Your path has crossed with those who are fated to assist you. They are more than friends. Confide in them. Remember, my hand is in yours. I will protect and guide you. Love will overcome all obstacles. Time will answer all questions." Waves of serenity filled Angela's mind and body, as though she was feeling absolute, pure love for the first time in her life. She wanted to grab and hold the sensation, never letting it out of her reach. She wanted to shout to the world of this feeling and share it so others would know of its existence. It was an experience of totality, all-consuming pleasure and contentment. Angela basked in the moment, unwilling to let it go, clutched it to her being, the music playing all the while.

RAVAGES OF ROSIE

Rosie Richards had no idea how she made it home, couldn't remember the ride or even driving for that matter. It was as though she was on automatic pilot. She had such high hopes of getting answers and a fast remedy for her skin condition. All she received was a prescription for some expensive ointment and an appointment with yet more doctors. Now parked in the driveway, she sat inside her car staring out the window, seeing nothing. The flowers she was so proud of, the lovely home she owned, the tangible evidence of the massive amount of income she brought in, it all meant nothing to her at that moment. All she could think of was the terrible, disgusting, scaly skin disfiguring her body.

She, who prided herself on wearing the finest clothes, having perfectly done hair, the most expensive perfumes, and the best manicures money could buy was dealing with something she had no control over whatsoever. It was more than her brain could handle; she felt completely numb. Her life had become a horror story. Rosie was too vain to share this with her friends or colleagues. No one but the medical doctors was going to see what her body had become, not if she could help it.

As Rosie exited her vehicle and walked toward the front door, a sweet voice rang in her ear. It was faint, yet clear as a bell, saying, "Ye be warned. Ye beware. Soon's a time you'll not prosper. Listen to me if ye dare." Childish laughter rang, followed by total silence. Not again, Rosie thought to herself. Perhaps it *was* a warning. Geez, Louise, look what I've been through since the first time I heard those words. A warning about what? And exactly what am I supposed to do to change it all?

As she stood in her living room, Rosie looked up toward the ceiling and in an exasperated tone of voice, yelled, "How am I supposed to know what you want me to do if you just talk in riddles? Beware of what? Listen to whom? I'm pleading with you to just tell me what it is you want of me. What is it you want me to do?" Not hearing a response, Rosie asked, "Can you hear me, Voice?"

Rosie was stunned when she heard the immediate response, "I hear you, Rosie Richards. You are asking me questions whose answers are to be found deep in your heart. You have all the answers you seek inside your very soul. It is not anyone who is 'doing' these things to you; it is you who have chosen this road."

"You're crazy!" Rosie replied in an arrogant tone of voice. "Who in their right mind would choose to have boils on their face and skin like a rattlesnake? You stop whatever voodoo or magic potions you're using right this minute. Do you hear me? Because if you don't, I'll find out who you are and sue your ass off! Nobody, I mean nobody, treats Rosie Richards this way. I got the money to take you through the court system and make your life miserable for years, you got that? I know this is some secret setup with hidden microphones or something, and I'll get you. I'll find you out and then we'll see who has the answers. Do I make myself perfectly clear to you?"

Hearing no response this time, Rosie screamed at the top of her lungs, "I'll get you if it is the last thing I do in life. That's a promise. Now, if you know what's good for you, you'll take this stuff off my body and leave me the hell alone! You'll be sorry if you cross me. Many have tried and paid the price. Did you get that? Did you hear me, Voice?"

The answer was a deep, disgusted sigh.

She knew there had to be microphones hidden somewhere. With great zeal, Rosie tore through her living room, turning over every cushion, inspecting each nook and cranny, hurling books on the floor, looking under chairs, inspecting every inch of the room until she was too exhausted to pursue the hunt. She plopped herself down on the sofa and let out an earsplitting screech. Her arms, her legs — every inch of her body was now covered with scaly, greenish-brown skin.

PART III

SOULS EXPOSED

A selected few,
Live amidst the mass
Of destructive view.

As they toil and work
For humanity,

Behind the scenes,
Into the night,
Emitting, oh such brilliant light.

-Monica Brinkman, 2009

A TRIO OF TRUTH

They sat on the floor facing each other, Karman and Angela's legs wrapped in yoga-like lotus positions, Euclid with the casted leg stretched out in front of him. Angela instructed them to be silent, open their minds, and give in to the experience. At first, they were hesitant to admit to one another they were hearing anything out of the ordinary.

Euclid perceived the sound of magical music, not of this earthly plane, and saw a vision so wonderful he knew he must follow the voice's words and reach out to Angela and Karman.

Karman sensed the need for meditation yet was reluctant to bring the subject up with Euclid and Angela, lest they chide or ridicule her. Then the most beautiful, enchanting sounds filled her ears. There were no words to describe how it filled her soul with warmth, love, peace, and possibilities. She saw in her mind's eye the wonders the three, together, could accomplish, and realized it must happen right away, right now.

Angela had been hearing the music for some time. Weeks, in fact.

It had been in her dreams and in her heart. She found herself humming the melody as she worked and went about her daily routine. The closest she was able to define the sounds was harps and flutes mixed with a pure, strong, soprano voice. The voice was not just one, but many, as if thousands of voices joined to produce the perfect sound. It was magical, thrilling, and delightful. There were no words but there were words. There was no beat and there was a constant beat. Such a mixture of opposites combined was unimaginable, yet it was so. And it was pure, untainted, love throbbing through every chord, every beat, every word.

She had been warned to allow Euclid and Karman time to understand the music and to come to her when they were ready. It hadn't taken long.

"Ya just don't know the pleasure it is for me to be in the company of such lovely ladies," Euclid said as he faced Angela and Karman. "I been thinkin' I was losin' my mind for a long while now. All I can say is how grateful old Euclid is to finally realize t'was meant to be. Couldn't resist, not in a million years."

Angela laughed, not in mockery but in understanding and agreement. She grabbed Euclid's large rough hand in hers, gave it a gentle squeeze while she stared into his glistening eyes. *What a sparkle those eyes now hold. It's as if they belong to a young boy, eager to delve deep into life and all it holds.*

Karman adjusted her weight, shifted from side to side until she found a comfortable position. She wasn't accustomed to sitting in such a manner but found it relaxing once she found her correct balance. Karman sat silent awaiting Angela's response. In fact, she intuitively knew to follow Angela's lead, to listen to her words and, yes, being analytically-minded, to thoroughly dissect it all before taking action.

As though she heard Karman's thoughts, Angela began, "My friends, I am positive you have many questions. Listen keenly to what I am about to tell you, but first you must vow, before all that is good and meaningful, you will not share my words with anyone else. Is that clear? Are you able to make such a vow and uphold it?"

Euclid clutched Karman's hand, turned his face toward hers and peered deep into her eyes. He couldn't help but think what beautiful brown eyes she had and how lucky he was to again feel so close to another person, especially a female. He'd missed this type of intimacy since the passing of his wife. Not sexual; the type of comfort only a good woman could give. A broad grin filled Euclid's face and he was happy to see it returned as Karman lowered her eyes and smiled back.

Angela had just seen her two new friends grow closer. She was quite pleased to see Euclid smiling again and Karman receiving much needed attention.

"Okay, you two, what's it going to be? Are you in for the long haul or what?" Angela inquired with a touch of humor. She was also looking for serious commitment from the two friends.

"Of course, we're in," Karman told her. "You're not going to get rid of us that easy, right Euclid?"

Euclid laughed as he looked from Angela to Karman. "Well, ladies, as I said before, it's been a long time since I've had the pleasure of being with such purty women. I'd have to have my head examined again if I said no, wouldn't I?"

Angela drew closer to them, leaned forward, paused for a moment, and, selecting her words with care, began to reveal the secrets she had been hiding. Euclid and Karman listened intently, occasionally nodding their head in understanding.

Angela broke the spell and announced it was time they took a nap for an hour or so. There was much work ahead for them, and it wouldn't hurt to re-energize. Also, Euclid certainly could use a small dose of medication to ease his pain.

"So, we agree? Take a nap, freshen up and then a bite to eat," Angela reiterated.

"That's the best news I've heard all day," Euclid teased, giving Karman a wink. Karman blushed.

Angela brought out extra blankets and pillows she kept stored in her office cabinet and handed one to each of her friends. "You can take the sofa or the recliner, if you'd like," Angela offered.

"No, Ang, me and Karman is just fine here on the floor," Euclid answered. He tenderly placed a pillow under Karman's head and covered her prone body with the thick blanket.

With a gleam in his eye, he gave Karman a pat on the rump. "You're as snug as a bug in a rug." Again that playful wink.

"You're just an old fool, Euclid Hannigan," Karman said with a laugh.

"I'll set the alarm for 2:00. Now get some rest," Angela advised as she nuzzled into the contours of the large brown leather sofa, her face set against the soft arm. Soon, the three drifted into slumber.

MOM MIRIAM

As in most small towns, the areas where the affluent resided were obvious. The massive, well-kept lawns, three-car garages, swimming pools, saunas, large acreage, and high square footage of each home left no doubt that the owners were well to do. The poor sections were equally obvious: the tiny, close-spaced houses, the majority of them in disrepair, most lacking the luxury of even a single-car garage, leaving their dirty, older model cars parked under the shelter of a carport or simply out in the elements.

It was in one of the latter areas of town that Miriam Grant stood by her soiled kitchen window, cell phone to her mouth. "Don't you understand that I have two small children?" Miriam asked, adding, "What is your name again?"

"It's John, Mrs. Grant," came the firm male voice in response.

"John, I need to feed my children. They require warmth in the cold night," she implored while rubbing her right hand over her face in exasperation. I'll have the money to you when I'm paid on Friday, I promise. Just don't turn off the electric, please, I'm begging you."

Miriam heard a long sigh from the other end. Then John responded, "Look, I may be going out on a limb, but if you can get the full $298.44, along with the late fee of $ 20.00, to me by the end of Friday, I'll see your electricity is not turned off. "

After a brief pause, Miriam exhaled in relief and then stated, "Yes, John, I will pay the amount in full along with the late fee. I promise."

"Now, Mrs. Grant, if you fail to make this payment or are late again, we will have no choice but to cut off the power, do you understand?"

"Yes, John, and I appreciate what you're doing for me. Thank you so much."

"Glad I could be of assistance. Is there anything else I can help you with today?"

"No, you've done enough. Have a wonderful day. Thanks again."

"You're quite welcome. Goodbye."

"Bye, John."

Miriam hung up the phone and turned to face her son, Timothy, as he bolted into the kitchen and headed toward the refrigerator.

"No you don't, young man, you'll ruin your appetite," she said as she grabbed him by the neck of his T-shirt, stopping him in his tracks. "Where is Tessa?"

As he broke free from her hold, Timothy looked up at his mother. He stuck his lower lip out in a pout, tilted his head a bit as a scowl took over his face and said, "Ah, Mommy, can't I have just one little itty bitty cookie? I'm hungry"

It broke her heart to have to tell him no, just as it always did. Truth was, she would have loved to allow one cookie. All they had left for dessert were two broken gingersnaps. "Timmy, my young handsome man, come here," Miriam beckoned as she opened her arms and pulled her ten-year-old son into them. "You don't need any cookies. You're so full of sugar Mommy's gonna eat you up right now," she teased, planting kisses across his face, still holding him tight. Miriam brushed a few stray blonde hairs from his forehead, gave it a kiss, and inquired once more, "Where is your sister? Didn't she come home with you?"

Timmy squirmed in her arms until Miriam let go. "Course she was with me. Think she went into her bedroom to change her clothes 'cause they were dirty." With exuberance, Timmy pleaded as he jumped up and down, "Can I ride my bike to the park? Mark and Chris said they're gonna go there and play baseball. Can I, Mom, huh, can I?"

Before Miriam could answer, Tessa entered the kitchen wearing white Capri pants and a gold and white T-shirt with *Super Star* written across the front in sparkling letters. Her dark brown hair was neatly combed and held away from her face with a narrow headband. What a contrast that dark brown hair was against her light skin.

Miriam knew her seven-year-old daughter was teased and taunted by many of the schoolchildren. Guess it was to be expected; children like to prey on the weak. Yet it broke her heart. Tessa didn't cry, or even complain, for that matter. But Miriam realized it hurt her little girl deeply.

Tessa walked over to Miriam, positioned her feet firmly on the floor and with one hand on her hip stated, "Mommy, I'm bored. Can I go out front and play? I'll be real careful not to fall or trip, I promise. Can I pleeeze, Mommy?"

Miriam gazed at her daughter and saw pure beauty where others would see only the gauze bandages covering her thin, tiny arms, legs, feet and hands. Most people who saw her believed the lovely little girl was a burn victim. *If only that were so*, Miriam thought to herself. Yes, that she could live with, knowing her Tessa would get better and grow to a ripe old age. Often she wondered why such a disease as Epidermolysis bullosa, E.B. for short, existed. For what purpose were these children born into this world? Their reality was constant pain and misery.

E.B. was a cruel trick of nature indeed. The doctors had explained that it had to do with genes that she and her late husband carried. Rather like Russian roulette. No one knew when, or if, a child would be born with E.B. There were no tests to find out if an adult had the gene, they'd told her — well, not until a child was born with E.B. Then the medical field was able to take DNA from the child and compare it against the parents'. Even then, she'd been told, the disease could simply be the result of a mutant gene that popped up out of nowhere.

In truth, the doctors knew very little about this genetic disease and as much as admitted that each afflicted child was, more or less, a training tool for the medical field. The extent of the disease varied from mild to extreme cases.

A tug at her sleeve interrupted her deep thoughts, Tessa pleaded, "Mommy, answer me. I want to go outside and play. Can I?"

At the same time, Timmy asked, "Yeah, Mom, can I go to the park or not?"

"Listen, you two, no one is going anywhere. Dinner will be ready in about ten minutes. Now go wash up, and, Timmy, get those clothes off. I don't want them ruined by your roughhousing, got it?"

Timmy let out a sigh of disappointment and answered, "Yes, I got it." His disappointment was soon replaced by laughter as Tessa pranced about the kitchen sticking her tongue out at Miriam and mimicking her words. "You children cannot go outside because we have to eat. You got it?" Tessa made the most hilarious face she could muster, puckering her lips, crossing her eyes, and staring at Timmy while she pointed a large spoon in his direction.

Miriam couldn't help but laugh along with her children. "You guys are nutty, you know that?" She gave them a wink and a broad smile.

"Now get out of those school clothes, Timmy. I don't want to have to tell you again. And, Tessa, you help me set the table, okay?"

Miriam knew she had the best kids in the world. Timmy loved his little sister with all his heart and protected her as best he was able. Several times he'd come home with a black eye or bloody nose. He would stand up to anyone who mocked Tessa or was cruel to her. She had told him to just let it go, turn the other cheek, consider the source, but nothing would change his determination to stick up for Tessa. What a stubborn young man he could be, she thought.

Then there was Tessa. Lord knows how that skinny little imp of a girl could endure the popping of the blisters that formed on her skin, the baths needed to keep her skin clean to prevent infection, let alone the looks and stares people gave her in passing. She was so strong in character, and she refused to allow the disease to take over her life. She lived each minute with zest and vitality, intent on doing everything herself without any help.

No, Tessa wanted nothing to do with pity. All she wanted was to belong, to be just like the other kids.

Miriam knew that to the world, her daughter was a freak. And she knew that Tessa was growing weary of the long stares, rude questions, and out and out gawking whenever she went out in public. Miriam felt like telling Tessa to give 'em the finger the next time an adult stood next to her gawking openly. That would serve 'em right, but two wrongs don't make a right, and it was better for Tessa to ignore them and not buy into their discourteousness. Miriam laughed to herself just thinking of Tessa lifting up that finger at some moron.

Again, her daughter's voice interrupted her thoughts. "Momma, I thought I was *helping* you set the table and now it's almost all done."

"Oh, sweetie, Momma's sorry. I was daydreaming. The table looks fantastic. Guess you'll just have to be the official table setter from now on," Miriam joked.

With all seriousness, Tessa answered, "Nu-uh, that isn't fair. I'll do it one day and Timmy can do it the next. Deal?"

"Deal for real," Miriam responded with a wink of her eye. She had learned to cherish the tender, loving moments spent with her daughter. Many times Miriam felt resentment that she had to be the one to inflict daily pain on the child. The baths were excruciating. Shouldn't be that a parent had to cause pain to her child. Just seemed to go against the law of nature. But it had to be done, and so she did it.

She shuddered at the thought of the feeding tubes children with Tessa's disease required to get nourishment. Come hell or high water, Miriam would do whatever it took to deter the progression. The doctors said she was doing everything right. In fact, they told her they learned more from her care of Tessa than they could ever teach her.

The oven timer rang, jolting Miriam back to the present. She walked to the stairs calling, "Timmy, get down here. Dinner's ready".

"Okay, Mom, be there in a second," he yelled down the stairs

She saw Tessa already sitting at her place at the table, obviously eager to ravish the little bit of food she was able to swallow. At times, her scarred, narrowed esophagus made it difficult to swallow. Then there was the ever-present fear of choking .

Miriam reached for the potholders hanging above the stove, bent over, opened the oven door and pulled out the meatloaf and potatoes, setting them in the center of the kitchen table. She watched as Timmy took his seat and for a brief moment found peace in the love that surrounded her little family.

After dinner, Timmy decided to watch television with his mom and Tessa. There was an animated movie about friendly aliens he had been waiting for, and it was coming on in a couple of minutes.

Tessa stretched out on a blanket set on the floor in front of the television while Timmy and Miriam opted for the comfort of the over-stuffed couch.

The air filled with laughter and shrieks of enthusiasm as the friendly aliens landed on planet Earth. "They're here," teased Timmy as he crept up on Tessa.

"Shhh, I want to hear this, Timmy. Be quiet."

Timmy settled next to Tessa on the floor, making occasional comments as the excitement of the movie mounted. In contrast, Tessa was silent, lost in the excitement of the tale. Brother, sister, and mother sat enthralled watching the aliens and Earth children save the world.

As the story ended, Timmy let out a happy, "Hurray, we won."

Tessa merely smiled.

"Timmy, it's time to get that homework done," stated Miriam as she clicked off the television. "Get your jammies on and then off to your room. I do not want to hear any music or shenanigans going on. I'm here if you have any questions or need help. Just give me a holler."

"All right," Timmy replied. "I hate homework, but at least it's not math today, it's social studies. We're studying the Civil War and I have to memorize the Gettysburg Address."

Miriam looked at Timmy and said, "Ah, Abraham Lincoln, one of my favorites."

"Mine, too," exclaimed Timmy, happy to share a mutual admiration with his mother.

As Timmy ran up the stairs reciting "Four score and seven years ago," Miriam could not help but chuckle. He was a character.

"Tessa, sweetie, do you have any homework?"

"No, Mama," Tessa happily replied. "We had a substitute teacher today and she didn't give us any."

No homework for Tessa was a relief to Miriam. It was time for the bathing ritual, something neither Tessa nor she looked forward to, a process that took two solid hours to complete. She had tried everything to cut the time down. As of now, that was her best time.

"Come on, Tess, let's get the bath done and those blisters popped."

Her eyes downcast, face sullen, Tessa reluctantly answered, "Okay, Mama."

Miriam was overwhelmed with sadness. She saw the apprehension in her daughter's face. They both knew what it entailed. No one with E.B. looks forward to the torturous pain of the bath. Miriam wished she could do more to ease the discomfort. She'd wracked her brain, but she'd not yet found a way.

The bath mat in place, Miriam turned on the faucet and ran the warm water.

"Okay, darling, step in."

Tessa grudgingly stepped into the bathtub while Miriam prepared the sterile needle required to puncture the blisters. It took concentration, since she had to tear the blisters rather than just prick a hole in them, to prevent them from refilling. It was a rigid routine of necessity. Each prick of the needle brought horrific pain to her little girl. The only way she got through it was to think of the results, not the procedure.

It was an act of love far greater than any she had known.

Later, after the children had gone to bed, Miriam cleaned up the dinner dishes, put them away and settled down in the maroon recliner. The recliner reminded her of Timothy, her late husband. How he loved that recliner. She refused to wash it as his smell could still be found on it if she pressed her nose deep into the fabric. She missed that masculine musky smell. She missed him. Lately she was also feeling anger toward him. How dare he die and leave her the responsibility of raising their children alone. How dare he be so thoughtless that he hadn't taken a life insurance policy out? How dare he go before her?

Miriam rested back in the recliner, picked up a magazine and started flipping through the pages; anything to get her mind off Timothy's death. She blinked once, then twice as letters began to rearrange themselves until they spelled out: Don't you worry because you lost your mate. Good things to come to those who wait. Your soul revealed will rule your fate.

Miriam shut her eyes tight and quickly reopened them. She stared at the open page and found it contained an article about weight loss, along with an advertisement for cologne and makeup.

As if she held a hot poker, Miriam tossed the magazine across the room where it hit the corner of the fireplace ledge and fell to the floor.

PAMELA'S LOT

Pamela Mitchell brushed her long caramel-colored bangs to the side as she sat at the dinner table surrounded by stacks of envelopes and letters. She didn't know how long she'd sat there staring at the endless piles of bills, most of which were past due. She had them sorted in piles by importance. The problem was, they were all important: mortgage, utilities, credit cards, medical bills.

Pamela wondered how she ever got into this financial mess and so quickly. Seemed there was nowhere to turn and no one who cared. This was her life now, one of hopelessness, helplessness, and humbleness, sparked with very rare bits of joy. That was the most difficult part of it all, the lack of joy. It was something she prided herself on, the ability to overcome all obstacles while retaining a belief in goodness and graciousness in the world. Now her days were full of desperation. She, who once gave to charity, who volunteered to help feed the homeless, who attended church faithfully each week was now the one in need. She did not like it one bit.

Pamela lifted all 110 pounds of her body off the chair, brushed the hair from her face again, knelt on the floor and, with hands together, eyes closed, and head bowed, prayed. She prayed harder and more intensely than she had ever prayed in her life. Her faith was somehow still intact, although the rest of her life was in shreds.

"Dearest Lord, this is Pamela Gilbert again. I implore you to lead me in the right direction, to hold my hand, guide me and show me the way to get out of this miserable state of affairs. Normally, you know I pray that you assist others. There are so many worse off than I, but, God, I find myself unable to cope with what's on my plate. I also find myself feeling guilty praying for your help, as you have already done so much for me. I'm cancer free now and I should be joyous, but I think that, perhaps, it would have been better had I died. Know that sounds awful, but the bills won't stop and I have no way to pay them. The harassing phone calls are driving me crazy. Why have you spared me only to bring me such misery? I don't understand, and just ask you to give me the strength to carry on. My parish is poor and has no resources to help me. I've no family, and my dear friends have done all they are able. It is now up to me alone. I don't know what to do or where to turn. I love you and thank you for listening to me, and trust you will show me the way. It has become too heavy of a load for me to bear alone and I am giving it up to you. Amen"

As Pamela got up calmness overcame her and she actually smiled, certain her prayers would be answered. Maybe not tomorrow or the next day, but surely she would find a solution. She wiped away her tears as she walked back toward the dinner table. Her cell phone played *We Are the World*, distracting her from the bills. She picked it up from the corner table and said hello. A strange voice stated, "I know you're crying, I know your plight. Just wait a bit and things'll be right."

"Who are you? Who is this?"

"My name means nothing. I'm nobody to you. Just believe what I say is honest and true," was the reply, followed by the oddest music she had ever heard in her entire life. It was clear and beautiful, without fault in tone or rhythm. It made her feel whole and good and perfect. But it didn't relieve her puzzlement.

Pamela stared at the cell phone in amazement, not fully comprehending what had just occurred. Rapid thoughts crossed her mind. This man said he knew her plight. So it had to be someone who knew of her illness and present situation. But who would call her in such a mysterious way? And if he was going to help her, why not come right out and say who he was? Maybe this guy was simply showing sympathy to give her hope. Never in her thirty-one years of life had she experienced such a bizarre message. She didn't quite know what to make of it and tried to push it to the back of her mind. There were more urgent issues to deal with at the moment: her bills. They were not going anywhere.

After writing the check for the mortgage, she collected the remaining bills, stacked them together and secured them with a rubber band. They would just have to wait until she could figure out a plan. Surely, someone would be able to give her better direction in dealing with her money matters. Pamela placed the stack of envelopes in the coffee table drawer. She sat down on the beige sofa, propped her feet up on the coffee table, and clicked on the TV.

For some reason her mind continued to wander back to last year. She liked to call it 'the year of growth'. She began the year healthy, free of spirit, and carefree, yet ended it appreciative, humble, and troubled.

Cancer, a word nobody wants to hear. She had tried to hide from the facts, from the reality that she could indeed die. Her doctor was blunt, telling her she could fight to live or give up and succumb to the disease. Of course, she chose the former option. She was one of the lucky ones who were able to have breast reconstruction performed after the operation. In fact, they were even able to save her nipple. What a glorious day it was when she found out she could have her own nipple, a part of her body she always took for granted, expecting it to always be there.

Now she took nothing for granted. Each day was a gift, each moment of life precious. Still, the medical bills had to be paid and life went on.

Being a freelance writer, she was fortunate enough to be able to work some during the time she underwent treatment. She wrote numerous articles for several magazines and was close to making quite a name for herself. Seemed she had a gift for words.

One thing she refused to give up was her volunteering. It gave her strength. Her philosophy had always been that if you gave of yourself to others, you received two-fold in return. Earning money was great but it could never equal the sensation that entered her soul when she'd done an act of kindness. Truth be told, she felt those were actually very selfish acts, done to help but to also feel that specific sense of overwhelming gratitude from those she aided. She cared very much for others but knew that without receiving that feeling she would never volunteer. It was a fair trade.

Tears filled her eyes as the memory of Tony welled in her mind. Tony Gadano, ah, he was the love of her life. Just thinking of those large dark brown eyes, thick wavy brown hair, and perfect body caused her to yearn for the sensual, passionate love between them.

He just couldn't handle the Big C. He wanted the perfect woman, the perfect body, the perfect wife. More than anything, he wanted tons of children. Her doctors warned her about getting pregnant. They felt she was a poor candidate and could jeopardize her health if she carried a child. What did they know? Did they expect her to throw away her future because of this one fact? She had refused and planned to have at least two children with Tony. Except Tony was not willing to take the chance of having her miscarry or do further damage to her body. No amount of love in the world would change his mind. She heard, through the grapevine, he had found a 'good Italian woman' and was engaged to marry her in August. Bet they'll have children. I do want him to be happy but I still love my Anthony so, Pamela thought as the pain of lost love stabbed her heart.

Jingles, her female Angora cat, jumped onto her lap, turned around a time or two and sat looking her square in the face. She stroked Jingles' fluffy white fur, peered into his oval blue kitty eyes and said, "Jing, what would I do without you? You've been such a wonderful friend to me, always listening to my troubles, and all you ask is food and love. Mommy loves her Jingles, you know that?"

As if she understood her master's emotions, Jingles licked Pamela's cheek and nuzzled her face against Pamela's left ear, purring all the while. She then took her place in Pamela's lap, rolled into a ball of fur, and enjoyed the continual stroking of her head and body. Cat and master were now lost in a mutual bond of affection and contentment.

For a brief moment, life was grand.

BRINGING BRIAN HOME

Douglas sat at his desk staring into the computer screen, unable to comprehend the information right in front of his face. "Concentrate, Doug, " he whispered. "You can do this." His head foggy and confused, he claimed the flu and hurried out the office door.

How long had it been since Brian was gone? Six, maybe seven days now? Perhaps he'd call the police inspector to see if they had any leads yet. He realized Detective Bruster had told him he'd call at the first sign of a lead, but Douglas couldn't just sit around and do nothing. It was driving him batty. Plus the guilt was tearing him apart. *Why wasn't I home protecting my son? Why did we let him walk the block to the park all alone?* Worse was the fact no one knew what had happened to his son. *Was he kidnapped? Was he being sexually abused? Or worse yet, was he dead, his body tossed like garbage into the river?*

His wife, Cheryl, had been crying her heart out ever since Brian's disappearance. She, of course, blamed herself. Why hadn't she gone with him to the park when he had asked her to? What kind of mother lets her little seven year old boy walk to the park all by himself? Would she ever see him again?

And that was their life, their existence since that dismal Thursday evening when Brian disappeared.

They'd been on TV begging for leads, for anyone to come forward who may have information on Brian's whereabouts. Cheryl had spoken directly to the kidnapper, assuming there was one. She pleaded with the person to bring him home. That was all she wanted, her son home safely and she'd ask no questions.

He couldn't watch the news as it ran their interview; it was too hard to watch his wife sobbing and pleading for their son's life. All he could do was hold her hand and let the grief flow. He had to let go of blaming her for the incident, though it was difficult to do. After all, she was the one who refused to take a simple walk to the park with her son, instead allowing him to go all alone. The poor kid. If he was still alive, he must be so afraid, wondering why mommy and daddy hadn't come to pick him up.

Detective Bruster picked up the ringing phone. "Bruster here, may I help you?"

"It's Doug, Douglas Payne. Any news on Brian?"

"Look, Doug, we're doing everything we possibly can do. The ten thousand dollar reward has been posted, we've scoured the woods, the rivers and the back streets as well as the main thoroughfares. An Amber Alert has gone out and my detectives are continuing to go door to door asking questions.

"Bruster, my wife and I can't live like this, doing nothing while each minute takes our son further away. There has to be something we can do or some avenue no one has tried."

Bruster's heart went out to this family but he'd seen it happen too many times before to allow his emotions to take over his job. Still, he knew he'd feel the same thing should one of his own children disappear. Hell, he'd be a real pain in the ass.

"Doug, what do you suggest we do that we aren't doing already?" he asked.

Bruster heard a long inhale of air followed by an exhale before Doug answered, "I have no idea what to try next. There has to be somebody who knows something or saw something, and we have to find them."

"Good to see we're in agreement on those facts," said the detective, adding, "It takes time, but I promise you that if there is anybody who has answers, we will locate them. We're not giving up on your son, Doug, you have my word."

"I know, Detective Bruster, just I'm going crazy and so is my wife. We can't eat, sleep or work. All we think about is finding Brian and bringing him home."

"That's my wish also. I'll call you when we get a lead and, Douglas, feel free to call me even if you just need to talk, okay?

"Will do, Detective. Thank you." And he hung up the phone.

Bruster had been working the children's unit for the last five years. Before this, he had been in homicide. Funny thing was, he found the children's unit much more difficult to handle emotionally. At thirty-three, he stood five foot eleven inches tall in his stocking feet, weighed a trim 160 pounds, and had been married to the same woman for fifteen years. He didn't know if their marriage would be strong enough to withstand one of their own children going missing. It was a tough spot and even tougher without any leads to go on. He pulled Brian's picture from the board, stared into the young boy's eyes, slammed his fist on the table, pressed the intercom button, barking, "Entwistle, get your butt up here pronto!"

***

"Come over here, Joseph, and sit by mother," instructed Lillian Darby, patting the couch cushion next to her. The young boy cast his eyes downward. "Did you hear me, young man? I said to get your smart-assed little butt over to this couch this second," she screamed hysterically.

Fear overtook him, and the young boy rose from his crouched position in the corner and walked over to the sofa, sitting next to her, but not so close as to touch her body. "Now that wasn't so hard, was it, sweetie?" she cooed. Repulsion overcame the young lad as Lillian grabbed him and gave him a large bear hug. She couldn't keep her hands off of him. He hated her touch. He hated her smell. He hated the name she gave him. But most of all, he hated her.

"My name is not Joseph, it's Brian, and you are not my mother," he said, looking directly into her eyes. Seeing her eyes change into slits, brows arched, Brian backed away. He'd gone too far this time and he knew it.

"You ungrateful little brat! How dare you speak to me in that tone of voice? How dare you defy me? I am your mother. Your name is Joseph and you love me," she screamed while shaking his body to and fro. "The sooner you get it into your head, the better. " Taking a glass from the end table, she handed it to Brian, instructing him to drink the contents.

"I will not," he cried out.

"You'll drink this stuff if I have to pour it down your throat. Now drink it this second". Brian gulped the liquid down as fast as possible, thinking it had a very strange taste. "That's my baby. That's my good boy, Joseph," Lillian whispered in his ear, as she pulled a blanket over his drugged sleeping body.

When he awoke some three hours later, darkness surrounded him except for a small slit of light coming from a weather-worn window which sat about four feet above his head. His legs were bound by metal cuffs and attached to a cage by large heavy metal links. "So, he thought as he groped his way around the circumference of the enclosure, she's put me in a cage. What's next? What is she going to do to me?"

It was cold and drafty with the outside air coming through cracks around the window frames. Brian felt around the cage, hoping he would find something to cover his shivering body. His eyes were becoming accustomed to the darkness and he saw a pile of cloth in the far corner. The chain allowed him to move about the cage but he could not stand up without hitting his head on the top. He rose, this time bent over, walked to the far corner and lifted the pile of cloth with both hands. It was an old shabby blanket but at that moment it was the most valuable gift in the world. Wrapping the blanket tightly around his small frame, he sat trembling with fear in the corner of his jail, tears running down his face, afraid of what would come next.

***

Every day at precisely 4:20 p.m, Lillian Darby made the fourteen minute walk from her house to the Riverview Park. She'd meticulously prepare herself, donning clean, fresh clothes, applying her makeup to attain what she thought was a natural look, and combing her short spiked hair into perfect style. Bits of purple streaked her bangs and brought out the brown of her eyes. She'd been diagnosed with bi-polar syndrome at the age of seventeen but controlled the extreme highs and lows of the disease with Lithium. When not taken properly, she would exhibit mania. At these times, Lillian came up with ideas and plans beyond her capabilities, riding the high and rush of excitement that ultimately ended when she reached the depressing low state of the ailment. That was the worst part of the imbalance, the depression. She'd attempted suicide four times and was hospitalized until the doctors found the correct dosage of medication to control her mania.

She hated the medication. It made her nauseous, dizzy, drowsy, and really put on the pounds. So, once she was on her own, she stopped taking the drugs as directed, only popping a pill when she felt her highs or lows were running out of control. Her life was empty, and for the most part she felt outcast from society. The one solace in her life was her love and gift of painting. Seemed she had an edge to her style that attracted art lovers; she'd been fortunate to open her own gallery the year she turned twenty-eight. The critics raved about the drama, feeling, and emotion her abstract works emitted. She mixed the idea of Fauvism with other styles to come up with what she called the Absolute Abstracts of Lillian Darby. Many art students tried to copy her unique style of painting but none had been successful in reproducing the sensations her artwork brought to the world. To date, she was still at the top of the list of outstanding painters.

From the outside, Lillian seemed professional, educated, and successful. But beneath the surface, she was a very sad, lonely, bitter woman. She had no one to love or call her own. Her need for affection grew with each passing day, until the ideal plan was formed and she began her daily walk to the Riverview Park.

TIME'S NOT ON OUR SIDE

"Euclid, Karman, wake up." Angela shook the shoulders of her comrades lying cuddled together on the carpeted floor.

Groggy from sleep, Karman opened one eye, then the other, as she became accustomed to the office lighting. She shifted her body upright with both hands firmly on the ground, arms extended. A loud snore from Euclid and they giggled like two schoolgirls.

"Stop that God-awful sound and get up. Rise and Shine," Karman commanded.

He let out a yawn, a snort, and opened his puffy eyes.

It took a moment for Euclid to become familiar with his surroundings; once done, he scooted his body forward, being careful not to place pressure on his casted leg. Even so, the flinch of pain was obvious.

"How are you doing, Euclid? Are you feeling much discomfort in that leg," questioned Angela.

"I'll be okay, Ang. Gotta learn to go without medicine sometime, right?"

"Don't be too brave. If you feel you need some relief, let me know."

"Will do, I promise. Just don't wanna be drugged. We gotta lot to do. Ain't that right, ladies?"

Angela and Karman shared a nod of mutual agreement.

"We'll get washed up. I have toiletries in the adjoining bathroom. Next, we'll eat before going to Karman's house. I'm famished."

"My house," questioned Karman, "why my place?"

"Always the inquirer, aren't you Karman?" kidded Angela. "All I've been told is we are to go to Karman's garden. There's an old oak tree surrounded by moss in the center of the garden; that's our next stop. Any problem with that, Karman?"

"Not at all, Ang. I was just asking." Karman stood to show Angela she was ready to meet any challenge.

After washing up, the three friends climbed into Angela's car and headed toward the restaurant. Once inside, they opted for breakfasts of eggs, sausage, biscuits and gravy, along with two carafes of black tea.

After stuffing themselves, the trio, now fully awake, wasted no time getting back on the road, anxious to carry out their undertaking.

Karman sat in the front seat beside Angela, giving directions to her home. Euclid had positioned his casted leg onto the back seat, leveraged by his good leg bent and placed firmly on the floorboard. Except for the directions given by Karman, the three remained silent throughout the drive, each lost in deep thought of what was to come.

"We're almost there," stated Karman, breaking the silence. "After this next stop light, turn right at the first street. My house is the yellow one, the third house on the left."

Angela followed the directions and pulled into the driveway in front of Karman's garage. As they exited the vehicle, the sharp barking of a dog could be heard from the back yard.

"Don't mind that racket, it's my dog Stranger. Excuse me for a minute, I need to feed him or he'll be fussing all day." Karman unlocked the front door, entered with Angela and Euclid right behind her. "Have a seat; the living room's over there," she said as she motioned to the right. "I'll tend to Stranger and be right back."

Euclid stood behind the three-cushioned brown sofa while Angela took a seat on the tan recliner in the far corner of the room. Awaiting Karman's return, each was lost in contemplation; Angela now realizing the responsibility bestowed upon her, and Euclid remembering Gina's last words.

Their thoughts were interrupted when Karman entered the living room, took a place next to Euclid and asked, "Are we ready to get this show on the road? Angela, you're in charge. What's next?"

Angela stood and looked at them. "From what I understand, we're to go to the oak tree, the one with much moss surrounding it. Once there, we will know what course of action to take. If you're both still up to doing this, Karman will lead us to the tree and we'll begin."

"Sounds good to me," Euclid eagerly responded. "You ready to do this, Karman?"

"Never more ready in my life," Karman stated and motioned them to follow her as she opened the sliding glass door which led to the back yard.

Though a dreary, overcast day, sunlight surrounded the tall oak. Bits of light illuminated the leaves, which glistened and sparkled, throwing off multi-colored brilliance in tones of red, gold, yellow, and bronze.

Angela sat on the soft mossy ground and extended her hands upward. Euclid and Karman joined her, one on either side, and they clasped hands. Once again, the music played in their heads. A soft, warm breeze kicked up and swirled around the tree, encasing them. Eyes closed, breathing shallow, the chosen three allowed their minds to go blank. Within seconds, their heads filled with visions of love, harmony, goodness, and grace. All negativity was gone, replaced by pure purpose and heartfelt ecstasy. The leaves of the giant oak blew with the rhythm of the mystical music, branches following the vibrations of the beat. A warm energy force encapsulated their minds and bodies as the karmic wheel turned yet another time.

INNOCENCE REWARDED

A vague, distant voice interrupted the beautiful music playing in her dreams. Tessa wanted to ignore it and listen to the angelic melody. The voice persisted and, still groggy with sleep, it took her twice to realize it was her mom calling for her to wake up.

"Tessa, honey, it's time to get up. Come on, sweetie, time to eat."

The young girl opened her mouth and yawned before answering, "I'll be down in a minute, Mommy."

Tessa slid from her bed and went to the hall bathroom. Something was not normal. She felt different, but why and how? After using the potty, she stood in front of the mirror and examined her face and head, then her hands, knees, elbows and feet. "Mommy, come here. Quick, it's important," Tessa shouted. When there was no response, she walked into the hallway, calling, "Mommy, mommy," until Miriam appeared at her side.

"Geez, Tessa, what's this racket about? They can hear you a mile away."

Miriam's jaw dropped, her eyes fixated upon the clear brilliance of her daughter's face. She grasped Tessa's hands while she examined every inch of visible skin from shoulder to fingertip. Tessa lowered her eyes and watched as her mother carefully removed the frayed bandages that covered her tiny thin arms.

Miriam, filled with joy, dropped to her knees, arms encircling Tessa's small waist and cried out, "Oh, my God," as tears welled in her eyes. Growing frantic with excitement, she tore the remaining dressings from Tessa's legs and body and removed the pink nightgown, allowing it to fall to the floor. Her lovely daughter stood naked before her, skin clear and free of boils, welts or scars.

All signs of the disease had vanished.

"How could this be?" thought Miriam. A ball of emotion grew in her throat and tears formed in her eyes.

"Mommy, what is it," questioned Tessa. "Don't cry. I'm okay."

"Sorry, Tessa, Mommy's just so happy. How do you feel? Does this hurt," asked Miriam as she put pressure on her daughter's forearm, expecting an instant mark followed by the ever-present boil. Nothing. Tessa's skin stayed smooth, healthy, and free of blemish.

"I feel wonderful, Mommy. That's why I called you. I don't feel sore at all. Momma, you have to see this. Look, I can swallow now and no hurting," Tessa stated with pride, allowing the saliva to flow into her esophagus. She then put pressure on her left knee. A small red mark appeared, fading within seconds. To mother and daughter's joy, the skin remained clear and fresh. Miriam continued to search her child's body, applying force, seeing small red marks appear and then vanish.

She didn't need a doctor to tell her that a true miracle had occurred. It made sense now. The words that had appeared in the magazine; the meaning so clear.

Clutching her daughter tightly, as she had never held her before, Miriam allowed the tears to flow freely. Her one hope and wish, now granted. Her prayers finally answered.

IT WARMS THE SOUL

Pamela lifted Jingles from her lap and set her on the floor. The cat stretched forward, hindquarters in the air, looked at her master and gave a couple of meows, making her displeasure at being disturbed from her comfortable spot known. Bending over, Pamela gave her baby a pat on the head and told her, "Sorry, Jings, but Mama has important matters to deal with." Mollified by the acknowledgement, Jingles jumped onto the sofa, circled twice before settling in, paws tucked under her body, head nestled into her chest. Try as she might to forget, the bills stayed on her mind. She hadn't checked her on-line account balance since Wednesday, two days prior. What she didn't need, couldn't afford, were any overdraft charges at the staggering sum of $37.50 each. As hard as she tried to be careful, she'd made mistakes in the past. So now she forced herself to look at the bitter truth before writing out a single check.

She rose, walked to the computer, and took a seat. Better now than never, she thought as she typed the bank address into her browser and hit enter. After she logged into her account, she clicked onto the nickname of 'My Money" and waited for her financial information to appear, unable to suppress a groan of doom, anticipating the worst. All she needed was enough money to handle the electric and phone bills, and leave her enough funds to make it through the week. "Please, God, see me through this," Pamela muttered under her breathe.

Her mouth opened wide and her eyes grew double in size as she examined the available balance of the checking account. There it was, in plain view, the shocking amount of $15,600.00. The last time she'd looked, there was a measly $600.00, and with her mortgage payment of $498.66, there had been little left to cover her remaining debts. Dare she believe this to be anything but a major bank goof? There was no other explanation than that the bank had deposited someone else's funds into her account.

It was after hours, but she could reach someone at the bank tomorrow morning and get the entire matter straightened out. In the meantime, she couldn't help but chuckle; just another of life's ironic jokes.

Tonight she would sleep well. Be it reality or fantasy, at the moment she had money. More money than she'd had in her entire working life.

And sleep she did, a deep, relaxing sleep with dreams full of cheer and hope, broken by that odd message, *I know you're crying, I know your plight. Just wait a bit and things'll be right. My name means nothing; I'm nobody to you. Just believe what I say is honest and true.*

Pamela bolted upright in bed; the words lingered in her mind. Tranquility filled her entire soul. She felt as if a heavy burden had been lifted from her shoulders and leaned back upon the firm pillows against the headboard, lost in the pleasure of the moment.

Jingles jumped upon the bed and rubbed her fluffy head against Pamela's arm; it was time for food. "Okay, Jing, I get the message. Up and at 'em," Pamela stated to her beloved pet. As she entered the kitchen she noticed it was 9:30 a.m. No wonder Jingles was so persistent in wanting food. She couldn't remember the last time she had slept so late.

After getting the coffee made and washing up, Pamela was eager to contact her bank and get the accurate account balance. Having that much money available made it too tempting to pay all her outstanding bills. Better to get it fixed as soon as possible. She sat at the kitchen table, took a large gulp of coffee, and then pushed the bank's customer service number on her cell phone, hands shaking with each stroke.

The first thing she heard was the all too familiar recording: push 1 for payment information, push 2 for account balance, until she was given the choice to push 4 for customer service. Once selected, a recording came on stating that *All available customer service agents are assisting other customers, please hold for the next available agent. To expedite your request and to verify your account, please enter your personal pin number and account number.*

After following the instructions, Pamela nervously tapped the table top, anxious to speak with her local bank representative. Within four minutes, a woman responded, saying, "Hello, welcome to YUR Bank Customer Service, my name is Brenda. Please verify your name, current address, and the last four numbers of your social security number."

Once Pamela provided the necessary information, Brenda stated, "Hello, Ms. Mitchell, how may I assist you today?"

"I wish to confirm my current checking account balance. I believe it is in error."

In a perky voice, Brenda said, "Just one moment while I bring that up."

Within seconds, though it seemed like hours to Pamela, Brenda informed her that the current balance was $15,600.00.

Pamela could not hold back a gasp of shock and inquired, "Miss, is there any way you can verify the deposit?"

"Certainly, Ms. Mitchell, hold one moment please."

Not wanting to be disappointed, Pamela held back the surge of excitement she felt.

Brenda returned to the phone and stated, "Ms. Mitchell, I show that a deposit was made yesterday afternoon, via money order, in the amount of $15,000.00, using the ATM machine. I can get a copy of the information on the money order, if you wish."

"Please do," answered Pamela.

While she waited, questions popped into Pamela's head. Could this be real? Was this happening? Who would deposit that much money into her account? It had to be too good to be true.

Brenda's voice interrupted her train of thought, advising, "All I can tell you is it shows you purchased the money order at WelcomeMart on Bishop Avenue yesterday morning at 10:17 a.m. As I said previously, it was deposited into the ATM yesterday afternoon. I see the time of the deposit was 1:23 p.m." The customer service representative then asked, "May I assist you with anything else today, Ms. Mitchell?"

This time, Pamela allowed exhilaration and excitement to color her tone. "No, that's all I needed, thank you, Brenda."

Pamela flipped the cell phone shut as tears of joy streamed down her face.

LILLIAN'S OBSESSION

She'd been coming to the park for over three months now and had made friends with the parents who accompanied their children. They found Lillian to be very sweet, intelligent, and caring towards their sons and daughters. She'd bring along special treats of fruit and candy or toys to stimulate the children's young minds. Many a parent watched in awe while their child sat intently listening to the story Lillian read with such feeling the child was caught up in the make-believe world of the tale. And when she brought her crayons or paints, the children surrounded her, unable to suppress the enthusiasm artwork stirred within their souls.

She was tender, loving, and seemed to enjoy the role of babysitter which the parents encouraged, allowing them a much needed break from parenting. They'd keep an eye on their children while relaxing in the warm sunlight or chatting among themselves. After a while, many allowed their children to go to the park alone, knowing Lillian would be there to watch over them, assured they had found the perfect companion in their absence.

***

It was a warm winter day, the time of year when winter waned into not-quite-spring. Lillian arrived at the park, sat on a green painted metal bench and canvassed the area, seeking one particular child. She waited patiently until 5:30 p.m. when she decided he would not arrive, so she began stuffing the story books and toys back into a large gray duffel bag. The bag half packed, she heard footsteps on the concrete slab as Brian Payne approached her.

"You gonna leave now?" asked Brian.

Lillian's heart beat rapidly with excitement and she turned toward the young boy, saying, "Well, Brian, I was waiting for you and thought you weren't coming to the park today, so, yes, I was packing up to go home."

Disappointment showed on his face as he asked, "Can't you stay a little longer, Mrs. Darby?"

"That's *Ms.* Darby, Brian, and I do have to get home. Hey, I have a great idea. Why don't you come home with me today? We could paint and play at my house. Besides, it's starting to get a bit cold out here. I'll make you some hot chocolate to warm your bones. What do you say, Brian? You want to come visit?"

Brian shuffled his feet and puckered his lips, weighing what choice he should make. His mom had told him to never go anywhere with strangers. But Mrs. Darby wasn't a stranger. In fact, his mom had told him he could play with her anytime he was at the park. His mom knew her 'cause they talked to each other when his mother went to the park with him. Besides, that hot chocolate sure sounded good. "I guess it would be okay. Sure. Is your house far from here?,"

"Just a hop, skip and a jump," Lillian teased.

Taking his small hand in hers, Lillian led him to her home. Her exhilaration and excitement grew. This happy, smiling young man would soon be all hers.

Once they arrived, Lillian allowed Brian to take a look around and become familiar with his surroundings. He had not been in such a grand home before. It was expansive, with one room for watching TV, one room for playing with toys, one just for painting, and yet another room set up with a projection screen just for watching movies. That room even had seats just like in the movie theater, and there was a popcorn machine and a soda dispenser. And she had three bathrooms. Big ones, too, with a bathtub, shower, and sink and plenty of room for cabinets and a seat.

She showed him one room that was painted all in blue and white. It had a double bed with a mahogany headboard and footboard. There were cowboy hats strewn all over the coverlet, each a different color and style. A giant mechanical horse stood in one corner of the room, the kind you could put money in and ride, except this one didn't have any slot for coins or anything.

Brian's eyes widened in awe as he took in his surroundings and found small toy horses, trains, video games, and a computer set on various tables and shelves in the room. He wondered if his mom might let him stay overnight sometime or maybe even spend the weekend. This was awesome!

After his initial excitement subsided, Lillian beckoned Brian to the kitchen where they drank hot chocolate with whipped cream on top and ate butter cookies. Brian babbled on about wanting to watch a movie or play a video on the computer or ride the horse in the blue room. Lillian had to tell him to slow down and close his mouth and chew his food. He'd have plenty of time to do anything he wished, but for now he needed to drink his hot chocolate and eat his cookies. Brian did as she told him but wondered what she meant about him having plenty of time. He knew he had to be home soon or he'd be in big trouble. He wasn't allowed to stay out after dark unless his parents were with him. After he had finished the snack and drink, he asked Lillian, "How much longer before it gets dark, 'cause I gotta be home before dark or I'll be in trouble."

"Don't you worry about that, sweetie," she assured him. "I've talked to your mother and she said you could stay here with me for a few days. Won't that be fun?"

"My mom said that? Oh, boy! I don't know what I want to do first. I want to do everything first, I guess," he said with a big smile on his face.

It had been a wonderful adventure for the first few days, except that when Brian asked to call his mom the answer was always no. Mrs. Darby would tell him she had spoken with his mother and there was no need for him to call her. That didn't sit well with Brian; he missed his mom and dad. Sure, it was fun playing with all the awesome stuff here, but he was beginning to miss his own home and his own mom.

On the fifth day of his visit, he asked to go home. Before he knew what hit him, Lillian smacked him across the mouth, telling him what a spoiled, ungrateful little brat he was and how he should feel privileged to be a guest in her home. When he whined and cried, she dragged him by the arm into the living room and forced him to drink some apple juice that had a sour taste to it. He'd felt drowsy soon after and fell asleep on the sofa. When he woke, all he could think about was getting out of there and going home. He looked for any sign of Mrs. Darby and, when he felt safe to do so, tiptoed over to the phone to call home. Except the phone was broken or something, because when he pushed the numbers, nothing happened. He didn't even hear any dial tone. Next, he tried the front door, but it wouldn't open no matter how hard he tried to turn the knob. Same thing happened with the kitchen door, back entry door, and all the patio doors within the house. Even the windows were secured tightly.

Little did he know that Lillian was watching his every move from a hidden TV monitor in her room. She'd carefully placed cameras in undetectable spots within each room. She couldn't help but laugh at his feeble attempts to escape, knowing he'd soon tire and give up. She could wait for as long as it took for Brian to realize he was now her son.

As the fifth day became the sixth and then the seventh day, Brian grew angry and withdrawn. He refused to play or watch TV. He wouldn't listen to her commands unless she used force or made him drink that sour-tasting apple juice. Sometimes the juice made him feel light headed, while other times it would make him fall asleep. He despised the juice and he despised her. All he wanted was his mommy and daddy back. He waited for the day Mrs. Darby would take him back home. Then she'd be in big doo-doo because he was going to tell on her. This one thought kept his hope alive and made it possible for him to get through each moment of the day. That was, until they had *The Talk*.

Lillian sat Brian at the kitchen table, placed a cereal bowl full of milk and Captain Crunch cereal before him. She told Brian that they had to have a talk and that something terrible had occurred. What now, thought Brian. What could be worse than being held prisoner?

He grew fearful and thought, "Maybe she's going to kill me or something."

"Now, Brian, I spoke with your parents today and they don't want you to come back home. They told me you were nothing but trouble and they are happy to be rid of such a bad child as yourself. It may be—"

"Just wait a minute," Brian interrupted, unable to stop the words flowing from his mouth. "You're a big fat liar. Liar, liar, pants on fire. My mommy and daddy love me. They'd never say anything like that." He began crying and as the tears filled his eyes, he said, "I'm not a bad boy. I'm a good boy. Mommy and daddy tell me how good I am. You're a bad person, Mrs. Darby."

Rage engulfed Lillian. This was not going to be as easy as she had planned. Certainly not with a high strung child such as Brian. She'd been too easy on this young boy and it was time to lay down the law, set the rules so he would understand who was in charge. She sat next to him, grabbed him by the scruff of his neck, turned his body toward her and in a firm, harsh voice told him, "Never are you to call me names. While you are a guest in my home, you will address me as Ms. Darby, got it?"

"Yes, ma'am, I mean Ms. Darby," he answered.

"From this day on, you will be referred to as Joseph Darby. You are now and have always been my son. Do you understand?"

Brian responded, "My name is not Joseph, it's Brian. And you will never be my mother. You're mean and a liar and I hate you." He screamed with such venom spit came out of the corner of his mouth, hitting Lillian in the upper forehead.

A quick slap across his face sent Brian reeling back, his chair falling from under him, spilling him to the floor.

"I am only going to ask you this once and you better have the correct answer if you don't want further punishment. Now, what is your name?"

"Bri—I mean ... Joseph," he said, his voice small and trembling.

"That's right. And who am I, Joseph?"

The little boy, once so happy to be in this house, sobbed, refusing to answer, eyes evading hers as he glanced to the side, seeking escape where there was none. He curled his knees to his chest, sliding his body across the room, stopping at a corner near the door.

Lillian scooped him up in her arms, held him out before her, a glazed, mad look in her eyes and screeched, "You better answer me this second or you'll regret it. Answer me! Answer me this minute!"

Tears running, his little face scrunched into a grimace and he answered, "You are my – my – mo – mother." Brian could not stop crying, his heart broken, his hopes now vanished.

"And another thing, Mr. Smarty Pants. Until I can trust you, you are not to leave my sight. Don't tempt me or you're in for much worse and that is a promise, you hear me?"

"Yes," came the reply.

"Yes, whom, Joseph?"

"Yes, mother," he whispered.

Hearing his words, Lillian drew the boy close to her body, hugging him, soothing him, and whispering back, "I love you so much Joseph. Please love me. I'll be the best mommy in the world. All you have to do is listen to me."

A wave of dread went through Brian's body. He was never going home. He wished she was dead. He wished he was dead, too.

That was when he first heard it, the music of the universe playing its symphony in his head. Such a magnificent melody it was that brought peace to his soul. It gave him much hope and the will to live. The means to survive.

PAYNES' PAIN

It had been fourteen days since their boy disappeared but it felt like a thousand years to Cheryl and Douglas Payne. They were at their wits' end. Every problem or hurdle they'd experienced in their lives to that point now felt insignificant. Bills, work, money, none of it mattered anymore. All that drove them was the possibility of being reunited with their boy.

Cheryl Payne simply existed each day. She cared less and less about how she looked, what clothes she wore, and had to be forced to eat. She was empty inside except for the all-consuming ache that would not go away. It was worse than any heartbreak or disappointment she'd ever known, and she knew that no one could understand how she felt unless they'd experienced the loss of a child. She needed answers. She saw the blame on Doug's face, though he was kind enough to keep those feelings to himself. They barely spoke to each other, and intimacy wasn't even on their radar. All that was important was Brian. Without him, she would surely die.

Douglas Payne knew he had to be strong in the face of despair. His wife had fallen apart. She had cried until there were no tears left and then turned into a zombie, not interested in life, staring blankly into space. He envied her in a way, her ability to hide within the confines of their home while he had to keep a stiff upper lip and live the life. Always on stage, showing a pleasant face to his co-workers, people on the street, at the grocery store, or the gas station. No one wanted to hear about his problems. They didn't know how to respond or what to say. How could they? He no longer heard "How are you doing, Doug?" or "What are your plans tonight?" or even "How's the wife?" No one dared ask him for fear of upsetting him. It was an embarrassing situation. So the people in his world remained silent and nodded their heads in acknowledgement instead of speaking to him.

At first, his best friend, Bernie, listened when Doug turned to him for comfort. All Bernie was able to muster was "They'll find him" and "We've got the best law enforcement agency in the county," but after a while, no words were adequate and all Bernie could do was listen. In all honesty, Bernie believed the boy would not be found or, if he was, he'd be found dead. Fourteen days was too long a time without any leads. The odds were against the boy coming home. His feelings showed in his eyes and on his face, so he turned away from Doug, fearful of being found out, ashamed of his own thoughts. Doug could feel Bernie's hopelessness, so he stayed away, only speaking with Bernie when he called.

When Doug arrived home, bringing hamburgers from the local fast food joint, he pulled Cheryl to the sofa and ate his food with gusto, while she merely took a couple of bites.

"Look, honey," he began, "you have to eat. You want to be strong when our boy comes home, don't you?

Cheryl stared into the blackness of her despair, seeing and hearing nothing.

He clicked on the TV, hoping to escape with a movie or show. Half listening to the re-run of *Two and a Half Men*, gazing at the motion on the screen, he came alert when it broke for commercial. There, before his eyes, were words in bright red and gold letters. They seemed to glow and pulsate: Don't give up. His time's not done. You will unite soon with your son.

What the hell? He blinked, expecting the words to be gone, a vanished figment of his imagination. But there they were, plain as day, blinking their message of encouragement. He turned away to see if Cheryl had noticed the message. To his amazement, Cheryl had a smile spread across her face and a single tear running down her cheek. She swayed back and forth, to and fro, as if following a melody. When he turned back to the TV screen, a commercial about a women's hygiene product was on the air.

His wife exclaimed, "Douglas, our boy's alive. I know it. Oh, thank God,"

"Did you see the words, Cheryl? Did you read the message?"

Cheryl moved closer to her husband, reached for him, and embraced the father of her child. She sobbed in his arms, her face pushed into the side of his neck. Lifting her head to look into his eyes, she laughed and said, "Yes, Doug, I saw the message and I heard the music. It was lovelier than an angel's harp, more beautiful than a concerto. It touched my heart and brought me peace of mind. It told me he is alive and that we'll see him again."

Could it be true, Doug wondered. Or were they so grief stricken they'd started to imagine the impossible? What he did know for certain was Cheryl believed she'd seen a prophecy and that the music had healed her soul. Even if it was imagination, for the time being he had his partner back, with a newfound hope and belief that they'd get Brian back. For this he was grateful.

PART IV

PIPER'S PAID

Now's the time to heed the words
that whisper in your ears.

You have the choice to make it right,
Don't give into your fears.

Are you brave enough to show
the substance of your soul?

The world strikes back with intensity,
To reach its final goal.

-Monica Brinkman, 2009

HAVE YOU SEEN ROSIE?

Dawn was approaching. Dew formed in the small town of Raleigh. It was a silent time, most residents still asleep. Only the servants of the people, the cashiers, fast-food employees, and gas station attendants would be found at their jobs, making preparations to take care of their customers' needs.

One woman stirred and shook her head to shake away the grogginess. For a few moments, Rosie Richards felt quite normal again, yesterday gone from her thoughts. Too soon, reality sunk into her brain as she scanned her body, now encased completely in brownish-green scales. When she attempted to rise from the couch, it was difficult, her body heavy, unfamiliar, and transformed. She peered downward to find her feet, such as they were, split into five thin finger-like claws. She drew her right arm into the air, afraid to look, yet more curious to see what, if anything, had transpired. Her hand, too, was now split into the five claw-like fingers; sharp nails protruded from the ends.

Rosie opened her mouth wide to yell for help. *He-iss-l-iss-p-iss.* She found, though crying in distress, her eyes produced no tears. *He-iss-l-iss-p-iss. The unformed words* echoed through the room as she tried, in vain, to call for assistance.

The last words Rosie heard before crashing hard onto the floor were, "It's not too late to change your course. Not if your soul can show remorse."

Her last thought ... *Go to hell.*

SLAVE TO HIS CAVE

Early in the morning, Angela had taken Monty to the After Hours Clinic, as promised. The physician, Dr. Kirk, took blood samples, questioned Monty on his eating and recent bowel movement history before coming up with the diagnosis that Monty had been sprayed by a skunk. Amidst Monty's protests, Dr. Kirk explained there was no other explanation for the strong smell his body was emitting. With the promise he'd run blood tests, he asked Monty to await a call from the Raleigh Medical Center Lab, wrote him a prescription to counteract the odor, and set up a follow up appointment for the following week.

Monty Frank found little comfort in the doctor's words. His wife had cast him out of their bed. The children avoided him like the plague. Even the family dog ran the other way. He was excluded from all family functions and exiled to the entertainment room within the garage. Hell, he couldn't stand the awful smell, either. In fact, it seemed to be getting worse with each passing hour.

Depressed, rejected, humiliated, and uncomfortable, Monty decided to make the best of his situation and settled into the recliner, clicked on the 73 inch widescreen TV, and prepared to enjoy the Rams football game, a six-pack of beer at his side. This year, the Rams were the worst team in the NFL, losing more games than even those sorry-assed Oakland Raiders, though it did please him that the Kansas City Chiefs had beat the Raiders' butts.

An itching sensation at the nape of his neck interrupted his concentration on the game. He shrugged it off for a while, until he could no longer ignore the need to scratch. His fingers curved, Monty gave in to the need but suddenly stopped when he felt something funny against his fingers. What the hell, he thought as he rubbed his hand against the newfound hair. It seemed the more he rubbed, the more fur he felt. He could feel it traveling down the sides of his neck, growing in density and length. "Angela, get in here, I need you to look at this," screamed Monty.

His plea went unanswered. Angela was gone, meeting with Euclid and Karman after leaving the children at the neighbor's.

Terrified, Monty watched the fur begin to cover his chest and arms, until his body was draped in a luxurious black and white pelt. Worst yet, the skunk smell was overpowering. So strong was the odor, it brought him to his knees, dizzy. He collapsed against the recliner. Before his senses left him entirely, he was aware of strange music and a soft voice saying, "There is hope to meet your needs. Transform your soul. Reform your deeds."

JOSHUA'S VOYAGE

Saliva dripped from the corners of his fur-covered mouth and fell onto his lap as Joshua sat cross-legged on the hallway floor. His eyes, now mere slits, focused on the abundance of hair which covered his hands and forearms. His once brilliant mind had become a foggy haze. His body, once so strong, grew weary and frail.

Through the murkiness of his brain, thoughts of his forgotten past surfaced. His mother and father, intent on consuming alcohol until they fell into a drunken stupor. Laughter and ridicule by schoolmates over his tattered, frayed clothes, purchased at the local thrift store. The bullies who took delight in pushing his thin, scrawny body against the hard metal surface of the lockers. "Allen, schmallen, you sure are smellin'; if ya know what's smart, better be no tellin," came the harsh memory-voices as he relived the pain he'd endured.

Through quivering lips, Joshua cried out in pain, "Please, not this. Whoever or whatever you are, make it go away." Howling sobs of anguish, held in for decades, tumbled from his mouth. *A-howl, ar-owl,* they echoed throughout the hall. *A-how, ar-owl, a-how, ar-owl.* Joshua noticed the fur — his fur! — matted from his tears and brushed it off, best he was able, given the paw-like fingers he now possessed.

The memories he'd put out of his mind for so long bombarded him, one after the other. There was nowhere to hide from his past, no refuge from the misery he felt. He was left with no choice but to recall and relive each excruciating moment, forced to experience the pain he'd ignored and hidden from his entire adult life.

Just when he believed he could stand no more, another memory would appear, jolting his mind until he cried out again and again. He shuddered, fur-covered hands against his face, no longer capable of shedding a single tear.

New images emerged of more recent scenes from his life. The harsh manner in which he treated his beloved sister, Beth, who had offered him only love. What did he give her in return? Abandonment, ridicule, judgment, and superiority. The pain of never being able to ask her forgiveness overwhelmed him. He knew he was to blame for her suicide.

He'd driven her to the brink of madness.

More pictures, showing how he had taken advantage of the good citizens of this town, caring only for his own well-being and leaving them to fend for themselves. Scenes flashed, fast and furious, of the wonderful, beautiful women he'd dated, bedded, and tossed aside. Their sweet faces, aglow with concern and affection, morphed into grimaces, scowls and frowns, their innocence lost, their hopes shattered, their dreams erased. Worse yet was the intense, excruciating pain felt. It was as though he was the victim of his own acts and deeds. His heart, which was breaking with the appearance of each new scenario, began to open. He tried but could not resist staring at the pictures now etched in this mind, telling their tales of despair. Despair he'd created as blackness took over his soul.

Emotions he had repressed for years he now felt: shame, guilt, dishonor, and, foremost, love. Love surrounded Joshua in strange waves of melody that beckoned him to follow its path to each note, chord, and rhythm. Harmonic tones pulsated through his mind and body, calling him to them. Joshua, though weak, rose from the floor and stood upright. His eyes had taken on a new glow; his heart, once cold, filled with joy. As the fur-covered figure exited his front door, following the music's path, a voice filled his ears.

Let it flow and be shown. Give of yourself; be not alone.

BRIAN'S ORDEAL

The young boy had tried his best to listen to Lillian. He really had. But he couldn't get used to calling her mother or acknowledging his new name of Joseph. Somehow he knew if he gave into her wishes, he would become that boy, her son. The thought of that happening made him sick to his stomach. So stubborn was he that he retaliated against her every chance he got. He couldn't help himself; the words simply poured from his lips: "I am not Joseph. I am Brian, Brian Payne," and "You'll never be my mother," and, the ultimate response, "I hate you," until she felt forced to pour that sour-tasting apple juice down his throat. Only then was he completely at her mercy.

Beatings became part of his life, so much he wouldn't even flinch from the pain. If he flinched, that meant she had won and he was weak. The trouble was, the beatings became more frequent and much more intense the longer he refused to cry out. His body was covered in black and blue bruises, though she was careful not to break any bones. If she did, he'd require medical attention, which was something she could not afford to let happen.

Lillian stopped taking her medication altogether and had succumbed to the low part of the bi-polar syndrome. So depressed was she that the energy she needed to fight Joseph did not exist. Her answer was to toss him in the large cage in the basement. While she wallowed in self-pity, Brian was unattended. He grew weak from the need of nourishment and dehydrated from the lack of water. Sanitation was another problem. He attempted to pee and poop in one specific area of the cage but in such an emaciated state as he'd reached, he'd wet his pants. The cage reeked of urine, soiled clothes, and dried excrement. He heard her moving around upstairs and called out in desperation, "Ms. Darby, please help me. I promise to be good and listen to you. Can you hear me, Ms. Darby?" Silence followed. Again he screamed out, "I'm hungry and thirsty. I swear I'll call you mother. Please, Mother, it's Joseph, and I'm starving." Again total silence, but, wait, he heard shuffling of drawers and chairs. "Oh, God, please have her bring me food," he prayed.

Within minutes, he heard the basement door open and light appeared in the darkness. His eyes squinted from the harshness of the sudden illumination. Brian watched as a disheveled, unkempt Lillian Darby made her way down the stairs. She shoved a plate in front of the cage, placing a glass of water with a straw sticking from the top at its side. Ravaged with hunger and thirst, Brian asked no questions, just pulled the turkey and cheese sandwich through the slot of the cage.

Never before had food tasted so good; never before had he enjoyed a meal so much. Like an animal feeding off its prey, he greedily consumed the food, making sure to drink the glass of water. He knew that to survive, he'd have to play by her stupid rules. He understood the game now.

MEMORIES LONG FORGOTTEN

Still cast against the recliner's edge, Monty Frank stirred and opened his eyes, focusing them, trying to become acclimated to the darkness. The skunky stench secreted from each pore of his body filled his nostrils with the gasp of each new breathe. Grabbing the arm of the chair, Monty hoisted himself into the seat, reached over and turned on the lamp perched on the end table beside him.

His stomach queasy, he fought back the vomit that rose in his throat and laid back into the recliner's welcoming confines. His stomach continued to churn, so much so he could not muster up enough energy to call out to see if Angela had returned. As he relaxed, eyes closed, distant memories once again appeared in his mind's eye.

A young, chubby boy holding his hand up as he waved it back and forth, his pleading eyes following his teacher's every movement, summoning her to glance his way, to acknowledge his distress. Oh, please, I got to go. I can't hold it any longer. There he sat, hand still in the air, while streams of warm, wet urine traveled down his pants leg and formed a puddle on the floor beneath his desk. Oh, how they laughed! The ridicule became too much to take and he went running out of the classroom, forever thereafter to be known as 'Frank the Skank'. No one befriended him.

Alone, he found refuge in the comfort of home-made apple pies, chocolate chip cookies, mashed potatoes, and, best of all, chocolate ice cream. He filled his hours in daydreams of what luscious treat would await him when he got home. Once there, he'd raid the refrigerator and cupboards, hiding his stash in his T-shirt before stealing away to his room where he gorged himself until his stomach hurt. It brought him such comfort, and the food never called him names; its only aim was to give him pleasure.

Images of classmates shunning him and calling him Monstrous Monty, Fatty Frank, Big Stupid, Smelly, Skanky Frank appeared before him. How it hurt to relive these scenes.

There he was, walking the halls of his high school, dejected, avoided, and ridiculed by all who passed him. It was pure misery and hell to be the geeky, fat outcast. He'd given up trying to figure out why they all hated him, but his childish reasoning told him he must be a horrid person for so many people to dislike him. Soon, he believed himself to be the person they said he was, a fat blob of worthlessness, a young man only a stupid dog would like. He blamed himself for the jabs and jeers thrown his way. Alone, he continued to find solace in food. He supposed his only real friend was Mr. Garner, who owned the 7-11 where he'd stop and buy his daily dose of donuts, candy, and chips. In fact, Mr. Garner would set his favorites aside, knowing he'd be in.

Flashback to twelfth grade: Butchie punching him in the stomach, calling him fat-ass and pussy again. Faces of his classmates gelled together, forming one mass of hysterical laughter as they egged Butchie on, saying, "Punch his lights out. You gotta hit him harder to get through all that blubber." Each new taunt hit yet another raw nerve. He saw this young version of himself rise up from the floor, glassy-eyed with rage.

Watching this vision, Monty wanted to cry out, "Don't do it. You'll regret it, Monty," but words would not form. All he could do was to think these thoughts and remember what followed. He cringed and tried to get the picture out of his mind by shutting his eyes tight. No use; he had nowhere to hide as the memory played itself out against tightly shut lids. The younger Monty drew back his fist and hit Butchie square in the nose. The crowd gasped, surprised fatso would retaliate. The blood dripping from his broken nose infuriated Butchie even more. He flew upon Monty with a vengeance, beating him unmercifully, socking him in the groin, bloodying his eyes, and, finally, pulling back two fingers of his right hand until Monty heard them crack. It was so bad even the classmates screamed at Butchie to stop. It was not until the principal arrived and pulled him off Monty that the brutal beating ended.

At that moment, the darkness went ever deeper into his soul until it enveloped every bit of his heart. He made a vow that when he got out of high school, no one would ever hurt him again. He'd remained true to his vow until now, when he was forced to watch the remembrances of days gone past.

Oh, the pain so deep inside! It was tearing him apart. His eyes felt as though jagged slivers of glass were penetrating their cores. Just when he thought he could endure no more, he heard it.

Wondrous music filled the air once again. Swirling, hypnotic, angelic tones of harmonic rhapsody played their melodies, whirling in his head, beckoning him to follow.

The intense pain disappeared, replaced by calmness. The sickening scenes from his past we now gone, replaced with peacefulness. And the music played on.

Monty raised his massive body from the recliner, full of hope and delight, eager to follow the path before him, his disgusting odor and blanket of hair forgotten.

ANOTHER TURN OF
THE WHEEL

The sound of evil laughter vibrated throughout the room. Startled, Rosie roused; her eyes searched the darkened space in an effort to pinpoint where this lunatic hilarity was coming from. A roar exploded through the air, lightning flashed before her, then it started: the music.

So violent were the chords, brutal heavy off-beat percussion and shrieks of violins in need of tuning. Thundering blasts of steel guitars played without rhythm as deep, harsh, bass voices chanted vile words of doom and disaster. Glass splintering mezzo soprano notes pierced her ears, while bottles on the bar burst into fragments to the floor. Rosie cowered and drew her body closer to the cushion of the couch. Her claw-like hands covered her ears in a vain attempt to shut out the incessant noise.

Hands reached out from the shadows, ripped the clothes from her body and tore them into shreds. She watched in horror as bolts of energy tore through her home and smacked against its walls, creating large, long cracks that grew ever larger until they ripped the walls apart, throwing sheetrock pieces into the air. The floor beneath her rolled in earthquake-like rumbles. TV, curio cabinet, pictures dropped amidst the rubble, all her treasures spilling forth in ruins. Mirrored walls were forced into surreal shapes as they inflated, deflated, then split into slivers of glass.

Rosie crawled toward the porch door, in fear for her life, reached for the handle and turned. She shrieked, "Hiss-elp, Hiss-elp." So weak the sound, no one heard. An explosive blast rocked the foundation and fireballs began to envelope her home. Rosie had no choice but to place one claw-like foot in front of the other and run to the safety of her front yard. She watched, devastated, while the home she cherished burst into flames.

Without a phone and unwilling to face the neighbors looking as she did, Rosie crept toward the garage, crawling through the gravel path. Once inside, she entered her car and huddled between the seats. Unable to outwardly express the deep pain within, all she could do was tremble and shake until fear turned into anger, anger into hate, hate into thoughts of revenge.

There she lay, cradled in the darkness. The dark music continued.

The firemen found a dazed, naked Rosie sitting upright in the back seat of her car, clutching her chest, carrying on about lizards and devils. Never again would Rosie Richards speak coherently. She'd live the remainder of her life within the confines of a controlled mental facility, rubbing her smooth, plump skin, babbling on about brown, and green scales, revealing the darkness of her soul.

BRIAN'S BACK IN TOWN

Cheryl Payne bolted upright in bed, turned to her husband and asked, "Can you hear that?"

"Hear what?" he answered gruffly, half-waking from his sleep.

"The music, Doug. I thought I'd dreamt it but it's still here. Shhh, listen, it's playing right now."

Doug shook the grogginess off, ears alert to hear what Cheryl was talking about. He heard nothing but silence and was about to write it off as Cheryl's overactive imagination when the first chord sounded in his ear. He was surprised by the clarity of tone. He'd never heard music like it, and lacked the words to describe the exact sound. Pure, soft, soothing voices mingled with instruments, each at the perfect pitch, as if a thousand voices intermingled to become one universal sound that touched so deep into his soul he felt a love unlike any other he'd ever experienced.

"Well, can you hear it Douglas," asked his wife. The softness of her voice blended perfectly with the melody.

Doug grinned from ear to ear, bursting with happiness and hope. "Yes, Cheryl. Isn't it wonderful?"

As if telling a story, the music instructed them to dress for the adventure to come. Without hesitation, they rose from the bed, showered, dressed, and entered the living room. Drawn to the TV, Doug clicked the remote, automatically putting on Channel 9. A group of chefs were preparing a variety of dessert dishes; inane programming, yet he and Cheryl could not stop staring at the screen. The program broke for a pledge drive, a woman requesting money to keep the station going, volunteers behind a desk, phone before them. As the camera scanned back to the woman, the screen went blue and letters began to appear. One by one, they came, until: *Don't give up. His time's not done. You will unite soon with your son.*

In the background they heard the sweet rapture of the music, beckoning them to follow its path. As if hypnotized, they rose, clasped hands and allowed the music to lead the way. It led them to their vehicle, down Highway 63 and into town toward the police station. There was no question in their minds about what they were to do. Maybe they were insane to go to the police with their story, but Doug and Cheryl knew it was their only hope.

They parked and walked the few feet to the police station, entered and walked up to the reception desk. A young dark-haired woman, talking on the phone, motioned she'd be with them in a minute. After finishing the call, she went to the window and asked how she could assist them. Douglas introduced himself and his wife and asked to meet with Detective Bruster. "I'll see if he's in," the young woman replied and turned to the intercom to page the officer. Within minutes, the detective appeared in the room and extended his arm to Doug for his usual welcoming handshake.

A bit embarrassed he had nothing new to share with the couple about their son, Bruster looked away and asked them to follow him to his office.

"Please have a seat," he instructed, pointing to two metal chairs sitting in front of his desk. He knew they were here for answers and he had none to provide. Better to get the uncomfortable moments over with. He had learned years ago to be frank. People saw through facades and trickery.

"I'm sorry to say we haven't had one lead as yet."

Cheryl piped in, "Oh, Detect—"

He cut off her words and continued, "Please, you must know that I am doing everything in my power to locate your boy. But it seems he up and vanished into thin air. No one saw him that day, nor did they see anything peculiar. Without an eye witness, it will be difficult to locate his whereabouts. I don't—

This time Doug cut off the detective. "Bruster, we're not here to complain or give you a hard time. We're here to help get my son back."

Taken aback, the Detective muttered, "Oh, sorry, Mr. and Mrs. Payne, I just assumed you were checking the status of our investigation. You know what assume means." He gave a weak chuckle. "Well, then, how can you help me?"

Cheryl and Douglas exchanged a quick look, Cheryl nodding for Doug to take the lead.

"Detective, before I begin I want your solemn promise you will not interrupt me. Let me finish what I have to say."

"That goes without saying," answered the detective.

"Perhaps in most cases, but not in this one, I'm afraid. My wife and I are as sane as you or anyone else, but we are also positive we have a way to find Brian. It's quite unconventional and may be hard to accept, but, if you're willing to oblige our idiosyncrasies, we honestly believe our son will be home today."

"Shoot. Give it to me," Detective Bruster replied.

Douglas took a deep breath, exhaled and went on, "For some unknown reason, a message has been sent to us. First it came via the TV and then in the form of music."

Bruster started to speak, but Cheryl reminded him of his promise to hear them out. The detective sat back against his seat and rolled his eyes, finding it difficult to remain silent after hearing such an outrageous story.

Cheryl put on her most feminine smile, leaned in toward Bruster and stated, "I realize we sound like we're looney tunes and if we hadn't experienced this ourselves, we'd feel exactly as you are now. But we did see the words, the message, and we did hear the music. In fact, it led us to your door."

Bruster held back a chuckle. He could see how serious they were and he had promised to listen. Suddenly a sound reached his ears, penetrated his mind and senses, and he no longer felt the Paynes insane. Now he was thinking he might be the one who was going crazy. He tried to ignore it but the music was breathtaking. In fact, it made him feel warm and cozy and free of stress.

Noticing the change in the detective, Cheryl asked, "You hear it, don't you?"

"Well, I hear something. Ah, was this music beautiful to the ear, perfect in tone and melody?"

"That's it exactly. It is so gloriously overwhelming you can't put the sound into words. The closest I can come is to say it is pure and total love. Wouldn't you agree," asked Cheryl.

"All right. It is as you say and, yes, I hear it, but what does that have to do with finding Brian?"

Doug laughed deeply before answering, "It has everything to do with Brian. Don't you see, it will lead us to where he is."

"That's preposterous! Why would you believe this music could do that?"

In a delicate, soft voice, Cheryl said, "Detective, we just know it to be so. It is what it is."

"Besides," Doug added, "what would be the harm? We certainly aren't getting anywhere doing nothing."

The detective swung around in his chair, flustered. He was willing to do this but he couldn't get a team together. For Christ's sake, they'd laugh in his face.

"Okay, folks, I'm in, but it'll just be myself going with you, understand?"

"Of course," Doug responded. "We wouldn't want it any other way."

***

It had been at least a day since Brian had eaten the turkey and cheese sandwich. His stomach growled and it hurt. Though he'd cried and begged, calling out, "Mother, it's Joseph, your son. Please bring me some water and food," adding for effect, "I love you mother," Lillian did not appear. In fact, he hadn't heard one bit of noise from upstairs for over half a day. He wondered if she had left the house. Yeah, big deal if she has, he thought to himself, I can't get out of this cage. He was so cold, hungry, thirsty, and outright miserable. Brian pulled the blanket tighter around his body, lay back on the hard cement floor and sighed. He couldn't even cry anymore. He had no tears left. Again the music filled his head, bringing hope and filling his heart with love. How in the midst of captivity he could smile was beyond his comprehension, but he did.

***

"I'll follow you folks, if that's okay," stated Bruster while walking toward the parked vehicles in the lot.

"Sounds like a good plan to us. That way, we can take our son directly home," Douglas said in agreement.

After settling in their car seats, buckling up and starting their vehicles, the trio allowed the music to lead the way. It took them past the Ridgeview Park, down Lynnwood Avenue and onto Kingshighway.

After traveling a few feet on Kingshighway, the music changed direction, taking them onto an unmarked street behind McDonald's. The area was immaculate with only four homes, two on either side of the street. As they approached the second house on the right at the end of the street, the music stopped.

Anxious to get inside the house, Detective Bruster clicked off his seat belt, flung open the driver's door, and rushed up the porch steps to the front doorway. He was soon joined by Cheryl and Douglas Payne. This was it; they knew the boy was inside. Bruster rapped on the door and could hear a faint rustling in response. He knew better than to dally and lose his suspect out the back. "Doug, get your butt to the rear door in case they make a quick exit."

"On my way, Bruster," was his answer.

Detective Bruster forced open the door with the weight of his body, splintering the encasement. He and Cheryl entered, the detective's gun drawn, ready for any unexpected surprises. From the rear, they heard Doug's voice, "No you don't, sister. Not so fast. Where is Brian? God help me, if you don't tell me where my boy is, I'll break your neck."

A woman's scream filled the air as Bruster and Cheryl rushed to the back door. There stood Doug with a woman's head in a wrestler's grip, held against his right side. It was obvious she was going nowhere. The detective walked rapidly to the woman, started reading her rights, and secured her wrists in handcuffs.

The woman raised her head and looked directly at Cheryl Payne.

Cheryl gasped. She knew this woman. Why, she was Lillian from the park. Surely she wouldn't kidnap a child!

Lillian curled her upper lip, spat on the ground and snarled, "Let go of me. What are you doing? What have I done?"

She screeched as Detective Bruster raised her arms, putting pressure on the tight handcuffs. "I swear lady, I'll break your wrists if you don't tell us where the kid is."

"Who are you looking for? The only child here is my son Joseph." Her eyes moved unconsciously in the direction of the basement.

Cheryl needed no further information. She knew where her boy was! She rushed to the basement door. When she opened the door leading down the stairs to the basement, she heard a cry, "Thank you, Mother. I knew you'd come. I've been real good."

She sighed with relief. It was Brian's voice, though weak. Finding the light switch, she turned it on and flew down the stairs. The sight before her stopped her in her tracks. There lay her son, surrounded by filth, a shoddy blanket covering his thin body. How her heart ached for him. What he must have gone through. She ran to his side, saying, "My baby! My precious boy! Are you okay, honey?"

Heavy footsteps sounded as Douglas Payne found his way to his son. His first thought was to kill the woman who caged their son like some wild animal. The second, pure joy and gratitude that they would be bringing Brian home alive. Never had he seen such a wonderful sight in his life. He rushed to join his wife in front of the cage.

After some less-than-gentle persuasion, Lillian gave up the keys to the cage and the cuffs around Brian's ankles. Pulling him out, Doug noticed the child's bruised eyes, mouth, arms and legs. Hatred rose in his throat and he turned to the evil woman who had inflicted pain on his son. He raised his hand to strike her, but was stopped by Detective Bruster.

"I know how you feel, Doug, but it will make things worse. You gather up your boy, get him to the medical center and I'll take the woman into the station. I'll be by shortly to take your son's statement and check to see how he's doing."

That was close, Doug thought and thanked Bruster for bringing him to his senses.

"Now get out of here." Bruster said, a broad smile across his face.

Though bruised, battered, dehydrated, and malnourished, Brian bounced back with the zest only a child possesses.

Lillian Darby was interrogated and copped to the kidnapping. Because she was bi-polar and in need of psychiatric treatment, the Paynes and the court agreed to drop the charges if she gave over legal guardianship to an attorney appointed to supervise her to insure she'd get the medical treatment she needed. He would see to it that she took her medication as prescribed, and see her therapist on a weekly basis, or more often if necessary.

Yes, it is strange how things work out, Cheryl often thought. At first, she and Doug wanted to see Lillian get the book thrown at her for what she made their son endure. But once they heard of her condition and the reason she'd taken their child being her need to find someone who loved her, the hate turned to sympathy. It might even eventually grow into love, she'd believed then, and it had been true. Forgiveness is a virtue, she reflected, but you don't always understand its importance until it becomes the hardest thing for you to do in your life.

Yes, it was truly a miracle that had occurred.

***

After intensive therapy, a controlled environment, and medication, Lillian Darby found the music, not of darkness but of light and harmony. It brought her peace, the love she always sought, and she ultimately became a pillar of society in the small rural town of Raleigh. She gave back more than she had ever taken, but the circle was not complete until the day she faced Brian, now a tall thirteen year old, and asked his forgiveness. The young handsome man searched Lillian's face before saying, "I see kindness and caring in your eyes. You're not the same person who abducted me when I was a young boy. Ms. Darby, don't you know I forgave you a long time ago? I'm proud now to call you a friend, a friend who contributes so much to the life of others." Brian had listened to his parents utter those words so many times, he could recite them by heart. He thought they served him well in his dealing with Lillian.

Lillian hugged him close, brushed the hair back from his face and whispered, "Thank you. I've waited years to hear that. Perhaps now I will be able to forgive myself."

She released her hold on the teenager, smiled, waved goodbye and walked away, toward her own life, her future.

PURPOSEFUL DAY

Still they sat, Angela, Karman and Euclid, hands intertwined, under the magnificence of the old oak tree, eyes closed, absorbing each melodic vibration. The music swirled in, around, through their very beings. Warm, brilliant rays of gold, purple, yellow, and blue shined down, illuminating every part of the mossy ground and reflected beams upon their faces. Crowds of people stood outside the house and pointed toward the sky in awe of such exquisite beauty. They fell to their knees, speechless, unable to form the right words to explain the magnificence. Cars were parked in the streets while drivers strained to get a glance of the evening lights. The melody, so smooth, eloquent, and magnificent, played in the air, riding the wind deep into the townspeople's souls.

Many people dropped to their knees in pure bliss. It no longer mattered: Christian, Buddhist, Muslim or Pagan, all felt the call. The music had no religion. It held the soul of the earth, the sky, the universe. Neighbor hugged neighbor without thought of position, race, or education. It was though they all shared the same heart.

Two silhouettes emerged from the distance and walked at a steady pace toward the luminous light, each led by their own specific symphony. They drew closer to the crowd, unaware of the fear and bewilderment their appearance created, lost within the confines of their heartsong.

Monty, covered in the thick black and white pelt, passed the growing mass of onlookers, emitting a revolting odor that stung their eyes and turned their stomachs. The crowd backed away in uncertainty, not sure how to react or respond. What on earth was this fur-covered creature, and why was this thing here on this miraculous night? Should they be afraid?

Monty managed a small moan when he passed the growing crowd. They shrank back in terror.

Shrieks of horror and shock filled the air as Joshua Allen made his appearance on the scene. The crowd rumbled, backing further away, powerless to avert their eyes from the advancing figure, uncertain if it were man or beast. Parents shielded their children, covering their eyes lest they glance in his direction. Hunters considered drawing their guns, but most stood silent and mute, mouths agape, eyes wide open, taking it all in. A few brave souls followed each deformed creature as they walked across the front lawn, around the side of the house, and made their way to a stop under the old oak tree.

The music intensified, growing louder with each chord, bursting forth from the three, Angela, Euclid and Karman. It came to rest within Monty and Joshua.

Angela was the first to speak. She rose, stood next to Joshua, clasped his face in her hands, looked deep into his eyes and said, "It is time, my friend, to allow others in. Time to show the world the goodness, grace, and purity of heart you have hidden for so long. Now is the moment to release all hatred, fear, greed, and lust and restore the natural order. Feel the energy reaching into your soul. It is a force that has been here since the beginning of time, ready to be given for the taking."

Joshua knelt on one knee, looked directly into the light, and howl-cried profound sobs of sorrow. *How-arr, How-arr.* The few who followed him into the area gasped in confusion as the black gobs of negativity, heartlessness, vanity, selfishness, and hatred spilled from his mouth and scurried into the dark. Simultaneously, patches of fur vanished from his body, bit by bit, section by section, until he stood before them once again a man. The on-lookers cheered as Joshua embraced Angela, then Karman, and finally Euclid. Joshua knew that never again would he allow his heart and soul to become hard. Oh, what plans he had in mind to assist his town and neighbors. He couldn't wait to begin, to reveal his true soul.

Monty had been silent, watching, hardly daring to hope, but still hoping with all his heart Angela would not turn him away. He questioned whether she would give him a second chance to redeem his true essence. Did she realize the years of pain and humiliation he'd suppressed or the wall he'd built to protect himself from others? Surely he would become the man she knew was deep within him, the man she would be proud to call father and husband.

In silent answer, Angela turned in his direction and smiled. She walked to his side, reached for his hand and clasped it tightly within her own. As she searched his face, peered into his familiar eyes, she asked, "My dear Monty, are you fearless enough to show the world your pain?

Are you humble enough to freely give of yourself to others without question or expectation? Can you release the darkness inside and exchange it for the music of the universe?"

Monty didn't skip a beat before he nodded in agreement. The symphonic melodic sound of music entered every pore of his body, traveling in and out and through; bright rays emerged from every minute opening as it cleansed him of all negative emotions: envy, superiority, self-indulgence, and gluttony. Huge puffs of brown gunk spilled from his body, filling the air with a rotten stench as they rose up into the atmosphere, faded, and disappeared into the vastness of the night.

He cried out in glorious exhilaration. The warmth of the music blanketed him with a peace and calm he had never experienced; it took over his soul.

The crowd had grown around the oak tree, Douglas, Cheryl, Brian, Pamela, Miriam, Tessa, and Timothy among them. They shouted and applauded in joy and wonder, for surely it *was* a miracle they had experienced. It brought them hope for a brighter future where each man or woman knew their purpose in life and each act of kindness would ultimately be noticed. They gathered around Joshua Allan and Monty Frank to celebrate their good fortune, the rebirth of their souls.

THE WHEEL SHALL BE AT REST

The music returned from whence it came, back into the universe. Silence filled the void, still Angela, Karman, Euclid, Joshua, and Monty remained. At their side stood Douglas, Cheryl, Brian, Pamela, Miriam, Tessa, and Timothy, for they had seen the ephemeral light and felt the music reach deep within their souls. They wanted to hold on to the moment, the sensation, the love of all things, forever. They held hands and swayed back and forth, to and fro to the music that now played only within their souls.

As the years went on, they spoke of that day often, that one day when they stood on the cusp of the future, and made their choices. But for now, fully in the moment, no words were necessary.

Euclid Hannigan held tight to Karman, the woman he hoped to one day marry, if she'd have him. Monty Frank embraced Angela with a new found intensity, inwardly vowing he would never take her grace for granted again. The vow was unnecessary as far as Angela was concerned. She knew Monty would be true to his soul, now free of darkness.

Joshua Allen had his own plan in mind, and excused himself after promising to keep in touch with his remarkable new friends. It was rather late to call Joansie, but what the heck, she was in for more surprises than just a phone call. God, he was nervous, but knew he'd wear her down until she couldn't say anything but yes when he offered his proposal. Besides, once she heard the music, she wouldn't be able to resist. Fact was, he wanted a family as well as a wife. He smiled, thinking how he'd broach *that* subject with Joansie.

Karman walked to Angela and said, "Well, my friend looks like we did something powerful and meaningful. But now it's over."

Angela turned, stared straight into Karman's eyes. "Over? Why would you think it's over?" She laughed, took Karman's hand in hers and stated, "Karman, I'm not allowing you and Euclid to get away that easy. Don't you know after all you've seen that it's only begun?"

**As one story ends,
Another begins**

Unique?

*Life's too short to take a stand
against another fellow man.*

*For when you delve deep inside
we're all the same
yet try to hide
our conformity
through
Foolishness and frivolity*

*when in the end,
We'll truly see,
I am you
and you are me*

-Monica Brinkman, 2009

*Be sure to visit Angela, Euclid and Karman
in the upcoming sequel*

THE WHEEL'S FINAL TURN

About the Author

Monica M. Brinkman, is a freelance fiction writer and poet.

Born and raised in the Philadelphia, PA area, she relocated to San Jose, CA, where she co-wrote and appeared in a small musical, How Lucky Can You Get. All proceeds were donated to The Muscular Dystrophy Association. She is a lover of all arts and has performed as a singer, actress, and voice of various radio commercials, along with dabbling in oil and acrylic painting.

She now resides in the St. Louis, Missouri area, which inspired her current fiction novel, The Turn of the Karmic Wheel.

In June of 2009, she released, Into the Tunnel of Darkness, a short poetry/prose book. It has received five-star reviews and was a featured book selection for the month of February 2010 on the Manic Readers site. You may find this book on-line at Barnes & Noble. She is a current member of The Writers Center and Writers3group.com., along with various other authors related groups and donates much time to reviewing new books for various Writers sites.

A few web-sites"
http://www.monicabrinkmanbooks.webs.com
http://americanauthor.webs.com/monicambrinkmanauthor.htm
http://www.redroom.com/member/monicambrinkman/
http://authorexcerpts.spruz.com/member/?p=9C2A0FE2-9087-4369-9D97-5EB9D3AB4CE0